A Taste of Charleston

Novel By

Tawayne D. Love

Dedication

To My Mother, Cynthia M. Love, and Angela Daniels.

The two of you have worked tirelessly on this, and I am deeply in your debt.

Acknowledgments

A journey of a thousand miles begins with the first-steps, and those first steps are owed to my mother, Cynthia Marie Love, and my father, Terry Wayne Triggs. It wasn't until later in life that I fully understood why you pushed me to get an education.

Getting these books together has taken a lot of work. Man, if only you knew. Nannette Chaffins, you know for a fact that had it not been for you and Mike-Mike (Author Michael Taylor out of the Nasty 'Nati) I'd of been dead in the water. Working from inside the two of you pushed me to do something I'd never done before. When we did I Am Sasha Fierce on my FB page I finally saw what the two of you had saw. Yeah, Chasing a Dream was a disaster, but it was a learning experience. For that, alone I'm thankful for my stint at Zitro Publications. From that, I learned what I needed to learn.

Angela Daniels, also known as Angela Tyree. You came through when I needed you. Trust and believe that one. With you and Momma by my side, we put all of this together. Thank you!

Hanifah (Weenah Burdette) if you thought I was going to forget the invaluable help you gave me you're sadly mistaken. Sadly! I know I drove you crazy, and I pray that I didn't drive you away, but I'm forever thankful for the help you gave in pushing me to learn more and more not only about writing, but about the business.

Woo Hoo stand up! To all of my peoples from my projects in Charleston, West Virginia. Thanks for the social media help. You helped me build my facebook page by your support and love. By making me relevant.

To my facebook friends. thank you for helping me make sure that everything was right with the covers, and making sure that the stories were tight. Your advice definitely came in handy. And thank you for pushing me.

And to you! Yeah, I'm talking to you! Thank you for supporting me. Thank you for bringing me into your home and giving me a moment of your time. I'd like to ask that if you like me you spread the word to your friends about me. The movement is just getting started, and there is no better salesman than a satisfied reader.

Contents

A Taste of Cream

A Taste of Cream
CHAPTER 1

LATOYA

"What?" I said into the phone that I now held with a death-grip, as I laid on my stomach in the bedroom of my one bedroom apartment paying absolutely no attention to the ten o'clock news. My best friend since our freshman year at Capital, Angie, had just told me she heard that my man, Michael, was messing around with Gina, this high-yellow skank from the Woo.

"Kim said so," she replied, and I closed my eyes and tried to take a deep breath, but couldn't. I was pissed beyond reason. We'd been a couple for the last eight-months, though the last two had been real rocky. This was the third time he had been linked with a woman other than me, and I was tired of it. I was way to fine to get played out by the likes of him. On top of being cute, and shapely, I had my own crib, my own car, and a nice job at the Kanawha County Clerk's Office as a Clerk's Assistant. He, on the other hand, lived with his mother and spent the night with me when I let him because I refused to let him move in until he got a steady job, which he hadn't the whole eight months we'd been together.

"I'll call you back," I said, and lowered the phone and ended the call without waiting on a reply. Kim was a good friend of ours, as well as good friends with that skank, Gina,

1

so if anyone knew about him creeping with her it would be Kim. On top of that, I was tired of his shit.

Getting up I went into the living room to get on the computer so I could get Gina's number off of Facebook. Logging on to Facebook, I went to my friend-list, got her number, and punched it into my phone.

"Hello," she said, after a few rings.

"Gina, this is LaToya, "I said, and took a deep-breath to calm myself.

"Hey girl, what's up with you?" she asked, with excitement in her voice.

"Wondering why you're fucking my man," I calmly replied.

"He can't be your man if you're not together," she replied, which kind of set me back on me heals. "You did put him out?" she asked. None of this was what I was expecting. I'm sure most of you have been through this before, so you know I was expecting her to deny it, and us to have to go down the dumb road of such and such told me until she finally admitted the truth.

"I never let him move in with me," I replied, now glad that I hadn't. "And for your information, we weren't broke-up, but we are now."

"I don't want him," she stated, and I could see her rolling her neck and the curl on the side of her face swaying with the roll.

"I figured that," I stated, cutting-off the rest of what she was saying. "Bitches in heat just wanna get fucked."

"Especially by an uppity hoes man," she stated, and laughed and hung-up before I could say anything else.

That's alright, laugh now I said to myself, as I dialed Michael's number. What she didn't know was that she had done me a favor by admitting it. Now I'd finally caught him and it was over.

"What's up with my cuddy buddy?" Michael sensually asked, when he answered the phone.

"Wondering why you're such a dog," I coldly replied.

"What did I do now," he wearily asked.

"You forgot to tell me we were broke up," I replied, adding, "or was that just something you told Gina just to get some?"

After a slight pause, he said, "you know you can't believe nothing she be talking about."

"What was you doing over her place last night?" I asked, and went on before he had a chance to formulate a reply, "or were you with one of her baby daddies?"

"I see you've got jokes," he replied, now trying to dodge my question.

"No, I'm just calling to tell you we're through," I replied, as a tear almost crested my eyelid. I'm not going to sit here and tell you a lie...I loved him. When he wanted to be he was a good man, but he didn't want to be anymore. And I was tired of being hurt.

"Over some shit a lying ass hoe said?" he asked the weary-tone now changed to one of disbelief.

"No, because I'm not going to let you, or anybody else, dog me," I replied. "I'll drop your stuff off over your mothers tomorrow," I said, and hung-up. I didn't want him to hear me cry, and that's exactly what I did no sooner than I hit the end-button.

CARLOS

Going into the washroom, I picked the block of soap up and washed my hands. Staring into the mirror, I smiled because tonight would be the last night I would be locked-up. I'd spent the last two-in-a-half years locked-up for selling drugs, doing most of my time at the Huttonsville Correctional Center. Tonight, at twelve-oh-one, I would be free with no parole.

Going to the back of the dorm where me and my dudes were all at clowning, no sooner than I made it back there Birch, my dude from Beckley, said, "Are you gone eat some pussy?"

"You gone eat that pussy," Shake said, while nodding his head. While I was gone, they must have started talking about eating pussy, because before I left we were talking about getting money.

"Not out the gate," I replied, while shaking my head. They all knew I didn't have a woman, though Shake, Coop, and LUD knew about my ex because we were all from Charleston. Shake and Coop even knew the story of why we broke up.

Dog, you haven't had none in almost three-years," Coop said, while grinning. "You better jack-off before you hit something. You don't wanna be a two-minute man, do you?"

"Fuck that, you got that penitentiary steel. Beat that pussy up," LUD said. "Watch, that bitch ain't gone go soft for a week."

"Shit, my shit got hard when the wind blew," Birch said, and we all laughed.

"I ain't doin no jackin'," I said, while looking at Coop like he was crazy

"Just keep it black," Old Man Black said, stretched-out on his bunk, which was right next to mines.

"Man, you've been down since eighty-five. That shit's so normal they don't even call it jungle-fever no more," Shake said, and we all fell-out laughing besides Old Man Black. He'd been down since '85, and it was 2017, so he was a bit behind on times.

"The only one that benefits from jungle fever is the white man," Black said.

"Everybody whose benefitted from jungle-fever please raise your hand," LUD jokingly stated, and everybody rose their hands besides me and Old Man Black. I'd never been with a white girl either.

"You've never been with a white girl?" Shake asked, a crazy-look now on his face. See ninety-eight percent of the people in West Virginia were white and the white girls were on brothers super-hard, so to find a black man who hadn't been with one was a rarity.

"Nah," I replied.

"I knew there was a reason I liked you, young brother," Black said, smiling.

"You just said you couldn't stand 'em last night," Birch pointed out.

"Came sniffin' around about my niece," Black said, which made me grin.

"How'd you manage that?" Shake asked.

"Yeah, how the hell did you pull that off?" LUD asked.

"I wasn't pressed," I replied, while shrugging a shoulder.

"With all of them pink-toes tossin' it around in the city you wasn't even curious?" Coop asked, smiling with a raised eyebrow.

"Is it any different than black?" I asked, now smiling.

"It isn't about being different, they're white," Coop replied, now getting hyped-up. He was into white-girls hard. He always said that it would be a white-girl that held you down during a bid, while the bad sister left when the sack was gone.

"So, just because they're white you should hit?" Black asked.

"You damn right," Shake replied, while Coop emphatically nodded his head.

"Gun 'em down. Gun 'em down," Birch chimed in.

"Dog," Shake said, now looking at me with a serious look on his face. "Don't knock it until you try it."

"That's what the butt-bandits say before they turn you out," Black sarcastically stated.

"You can knock that without trying it," Lud stated, and we all fell out laughing. I would really miss these dudes. This was like an every night thing, just sitting around clowning, but in a few hours, it would be over. In a few hours, I would be heading back to my city.

CHAPTER 2

CARLOS

Last night when I walked out of prison, my brother was there waiting on me with my Infinity. I'd held out hope that my ex, Scarlett, would be with him, but it didn't happen. K-Solo said that he had talked to her the day before and she'd told him she wanted to see me, but I guess not bad enough to come and pick me up, or be waiting on me when I hit the city. It was all good though. I had my side-chick, Lisa, waiting on me at the room and I beat her insides up for almost three-hours.

I'm a keep it real, at times I made love to her like she was Scarlett. Even though she shitted on me, I couldn't get her out of my system. It was cool though because Lisa deserved that. For the last six-months she'd held me down like she was my number one instead of us just being friends and fuck-buddies when I hit the streets.

Coming out of the bathroom, I saw Lisa's lithe, chocolate, naked body stretched out on the bed and my eyes roamed her body. She had dark-aureoles, darker even than her chocolate skin-complexion, with nipples a shade lighter. Seeing me looking she parted, her legs some and I looked upon her beautifully manicured woman-hood. She had that small triangle at the top, with the point ending at her clit. As if, the triangle pointed the way to her desire.

And she was beautiful. I forgot to tell you she was a Hooter-girl, and made enough from her job to have her own crib, dress nice, and send me twenty-five dollars a week. And that's not counting coming to see me twice a month for the whole weekend, and keeping the phone bill paid.

"Sooooo," she sensually purred, and looked me up and down, while parting her legs even more.

"You're trying to get me cussed out," I said, with a grin at the corner of my lips. She knew I had to catch my pops before he made it to work. He didn't even know I was home, so I was about to surprise him. He thought I was coming home next week.

"Just make sure you hurry back," she stated, and reached over and pulled the covers over herself just enough to cover her lower half, while still looking me up and down with that look that had my joint pushing the towel out.

"You got that," I said, and went to get dressed before I did what I really wanted to do, which was beat her back out again. Even though her sex-game wasn't on par with Scarlett's, she was definitely a genius.

LATOYA

Last night I cried myself to sleep, and this morning I awoke happy. And I mean genuinely happy. While getting myself together I was singing, and I couldn't remember the last time I'd sang in the morning. Michael had weighed me down with stress just that bad, but not anymore. It was over, and no amount of promises, or begging, could put us back together.

Clipping my earpiece to my ear, not caring that it was six-thirty in the morning and Angie was more than likely asleep; I dialed her number while getting my breakfast started. I didn't have to be at work until eight, so I had plenty of time to make me a nice breakfast.

"You are so wrong," Angie said, when she answered the call. She was more than likely talking about me turning my phone off last night, which I'd done right after I started crying.

"After talking to the hoe, I needed a minute to collect myself," I said, while opening the refrigerator.

"Who, Gina?"

"Yes," I replied, and told her about the conversation.

"You know I cussed her out on the 'book last night," she said.

"No, I haven't been on there," I replied, which I hadn't. "I'm done with Michael's drama though."

"And I gave his triflin' ass a piece of my mind too," she said, and I knew when I logged on I'd see last night's fireworks plastered all over everybody's walls.

"Girl, I'm so over that situation it's not even funny," I said, and my happiness was in my tone. And when I sang the hook to *"Unfoolish"*, she laughed on the other end.

That's my girl," she said, when I was done. "New chapter, and there's no better day to begin it on than Friday. You know it's going down in F.L.I.R.T.S. tonight."

"Why not the Indigo?" I asked. I'll be honest...I had ulterior motives. It was close to the West Side and I might bump into Gina.

"You're trying to have us up in there fighting the whole West Side," she said, which caused me to grin. "Leave that hoe alone, girl. She did you a favor."

"I know," I said, which I knew was true, though I still wanted to at least give her a piece of my mind. "F.L.I.R.T. S it is."

"Good, now I'm going back to sleep. Call me when you get off," she said, and we exchanged good-byes and hung-up.

CARLOS

My father lived over on Vine Street on the westside and that's where me and my brother were at about seven-thirty when he came out of the door of our two-story brick-house. It had been fourteen months since last I saw him. He had come to see me once while I was at Huttonsville and couldn't handle it.

We talked twice a week on the phone, and we wrote two or three-times a week, but he adamantly stated that he never wanted to see me like that again. This was my old man who had raised me since I was four after my mother died in a car-wreck, so we were really close. Making sure the door was locked he turned and started down the steps to the walkway leading to the fence when he caught sight of us leaning against K-Solo's Suburban.

"Sure, hope you don't think you fooled me into thinking you were coming home next week," he said, standing there on the porch. And I knew he was faking, just like he knew I knew he was faking. If he'd of known I was coming home last night, he would have been right there with K-Solo to get me.

"Cut the jokes," I stated, while leaning up and going through the gate, as he started down the walkway.

"Welcome home boy," he said, wrapping me up in a tight-hug.

"I missed you Pops," I said, with emotion in my voice.

"I missed you too," he stated.

"If 'err tear drops, I'm tellin you," K-Solo jokingly stated.

"You know I'm gettin you for this right?" Pops said, pointing a finger at K-Solo to emphasize his point as we released each other.

"Get him, this was his idea," K-Solo said, pointing at me.

"You to," Pops affectionately said to me. "You are going to be around when I get off, right?"

"K's taking us to dinner," I replied, nodding my head.

"Who?" K-Solo asked, now looking at me like I was tripping.

"You," Pops replied, with his customary easy grin, though his tone let it be known that that's what was going down.

"You got that," K-Solo said.

"I'll see the two of you when I come then, "Pops said, and draped his arm across my shoulder and we walked together towards his truck.

LATOYA

At nine o'clock, the Clerk's Office officially opened for business, but unofficially we opened at eight-thirty for court personnel. That's why, at ten-till nine, I was sitting at the

12

counter when Kyle came in. Kyle was a private investigator and a good one at that even though he worked for the Public Defender's Office. He was also white, twenty-five, and cute for a white-boy. He'd also been campaigning for me to let him take me out, but I always told him that I had a man even before Michael. He was a nice guy and all, but the truth would hurt.

"Hey Kyle," I said, as he came to my side of the counter.

"Hey, what's up with you?" he asked, as he waved at Dolly, the other assistant working the counter with me.

"Getting ready to open up," I replied. "Anything I can help you with?"

"How about dinner at The Caboose now that you're single?" he replied, and that caused me to look at him with a raised eyebrow for two reasons. Him knowing I was single and the invitation to The Caboose. The Caboose seated by reservation only, and the only time I'd ever eaten there it was four of us, and the check, including the tip, was a little over four-hundred dollars. And we didn't order a bottle of wine to go along with our meal. We each had two-glasses.

"And how do you know I'm single?" I asked.

"With all the trash talk that was going on last night," he replied, and he would have kept on going had I not cleared my throat loud enough to silence time. Leaning on the counter, with a half-grin on his face, he said "I just so happened to have reservations for two tonight."

"Sorry, tonight's girls' night out at F.L.I.R.T.S," I sympathetically replied.

"Can I have your number then?" he asked.

Thinking about it for a few seconds, I finally said, "give me yours and I'll call you before I go out."

"Alright," he replied, and took a card out of his shirt-pocket and handed it to me with the back facing me. Looking from me to the back it, and then back up at me, he said, "it's on your page. I was just being polite."

Looking down, I saw my number and my honey-brown complexion turned beet-red. He was telling me that he'd had my number the whole time, but wanted to be a gentleman and ask. Turning the card over so I could see his number, I handed him the card back and said, "Call me around six."

"Alright," he stated, and took the card while smiling from ear to ear.

CARLOS

"I'll call you when I get off," Lisa said, as I pulled to a stop in front of Hooter's.

"Alright," I said, and put the car in park.

Leaning over, she gave me one of those kisses that had me breathing a bit harder than I was before we started. "Welcome home babe," she sensually stated, while caressing my cheek.

"You definitely did that," I said while staring into her eyes.

"Are you spending the night with me?" she asked, and reached down to get her duffle bag from between her legs.

"Solo has something on deck after dinner with Pops. Depends on what that is," I replied. I wanted to hedge my bet in case I ran into something exclusive at the club tonight.

"I'll call you when I get off then," she said, and got out.

Waiting until she was inside, I pulled off while dialing Scarlett's number. Somehow, she had gotten my number, more than likely from K-Solo, and had sent me a text about an hour ago asking me to call her when I had time.

"Hi," she hesitantly said.

"You wanted me to call," I stated, my tone the same.

"Yes, I wanted to talk to you."

"What's up?" I asked, fighting to maintain my resolve. For thirty-eight months, this had been my heart until one of her girls poisoned her mind and told her that I'd been creeping with her cousin, Tiffany, causing her to go bananas. She'd had twenty-thousand dollars of my money put up so we would both be alright while I was away, along with all of my clothes and jewels and the keys to my whip and crib. Now everything was gone except for my car. And I didn't even dick her freaky-ass cousin down.

"Can you come to South Charleston?" she asked.

"Where at?" I asked before common sense got the better of me and I told her to beat it.

CHAPTER 3

CARLOS

Pulling into the driveway of the address Scarlett had given me, I turned the car off wondering whose house this was? The house was nice, redbrick, with a two-car garage. It was one-story, with a nice-yard in a very nice neighborhood, which was to be expected. Even the low-class housing development in South Charleston was upscale compared to the ones in Charleston. They didn't even call it a project down here.

Getting out, I went to the front door and started to knock, but stopped when the door swung open. As it swung open, in my mind I was envisioning her standing behind it naked. When it finally opened and I saw she wasn't, I was so far into my fantasy that I couldn't stop myself from looking her up and down. The first thing that caught my attention was that the twenty-months since last I saw her hadn't diminished her beauty in the least. She still looked like a slightly darker version of Karlie Red, with fuller breasts and a little less butt. And the white-pants and shirt she was wearing showed it off to perfection.

"Like what you see?" she asked, with a half-grin creasing her lips, as I came in and saw the living-room to my left and a hallway that looked like it lead to the kitchen straight ahead, while she shut the door.

Turning to look at her butt, I said, "I do now."

"That's funny, I always thought I looked better coming than going," she sarcastically stated, while locking the door and turning to lead the way into the living room.

Stopping her as she started around the couch, I said, "Whose crib is this?"

"Mines," she replied, while turning to face me while I looked around, this time seeing the whole living room instead of part of it, which was all I could see from the door. On the fireplace were pictures of her, and one of her parents.

"Who you messin with?" I asked, and I couldn't mask the hardedge in my tone, nor the intense look on my face.

"Nobody," she replied, in a hesitant-tone, and started to say something else, but I stepped into her, cupped the back of her head and molded my lips to hers. And it wasn't one of those tender-kisses either. It was jive-like a bruising one. And after a few-second of it, she was matching my intensity. She even started pulling at my shirt, so I went for the buttons on her pants and a minute or so later, we were both naked.

Turning her around, she bent over at the waist until her elbows were on the couch supporting her upper-body. Watching as she spread her legs, I don't think I'd ever been that horny in my life. Her ass looked so good bent over like that. Skin unblemished, cheeks just right, pussy with little wisps of brownish black-hair begging me to punish it. And I knew what was waiting on me if I spread them cheeks. And so, you know before it goes down I eat pussy and ass. Ain't no shame in my game, though it wasn't going down like that now? Right now I was about to lay this nine-iron, which was more like a seven-iron, but who was counting.

Grabbing Moby, which was the nickname I'd given him, by the base I stepped in behind her and placed him at the center of her woman-hood. Moving him up and down her slit, she moaned in anticipation of the dick and tried to back up on it, but caused him to slide down between her legs.

"You missed Moby, didn't you?" I asked, while lining him back up.

"I missed you," she replied, while looking over her shoulder at me, and I drove all of the way into her hot wetness to the hilt. If it wasn't for what I was doing I would've been pissed, but I was a sucker for some good pussy so there was no use frontin'.

"Ahhhh," I audibly moaned, eyes now closed, mouth slightly parted, with a look of bliss now on my face, as orgasmic tremors raced from Moby's head throughout my body. And when she started rocking on me, while doing whatever you women be doing with your inner-muscles, I wanted to tell her to hold on and let me get myself together, but I couldn't. It felt so good that all I could do was keep saying, "ahhh," while standing there with my hands on her hips looking stupid until those little tremors turned into big ones, and I started busting. It was then that my hips came to life, and I started driving in and out of her in jerky-motions, while I rode the ride. I'd never busted that fast before in my life, not even when I'd gotten my first piece. And I'm not telling you how quick it was either, but it was more than a minute and less than two-in-a-half. The good thing was that I was still hard as a rock so the show definitely wasn't over.

CARLOS

When I made it to Scarlett's it was a little after one. It was now a quarter-to-four and we were both stretched out on the couch breathing hard, as we basked in that after-sex glow while the air-conditioning dried the sweat from our bodies. Had it not been for my brothers untimely call I would of dozed off I was so exhausted.

"What's up," I tiredly said into the phone, as Scarlett stretched back out on top of me.

"Damn, you sound like you been gettin it in cause I know you're not about to lay it down and

Pops gets off at five," he said, and I started shaking the dredges of exhaustion off. "Where you at?"

"South Charleston," I replied, and he busted out laughing.

"I knew she was gone get you."

"Whatever Bra," I stated, though I did grin. "I'm a meet you at the crib at five."

"In a minute."

"In a minute," I stated, and hung up. Lokking to Scarlett, I said, "I need to take a quick shower."

"Can I take it with you?" she purred, and started lightly trailing the tips of her fingers up my arm.

"Won't be nothing quick about it if you do," I replied, and it took all I had not to cup a cheek and kiss her. She knew that was a turn-on for me. "I gotta meet Pops."

"Are we ever going to talk?" she asked, and that question had me in my body.

"Can I get my stuff back?" I asked, while motioning her to move so I could sit up. "I didn't fuck Tiff. I don't care what none of 'em said."

"If I had it I'd give it back to you, even though I don't believe you," she replied, and I just looked at her and shook my head. "You can come and live with me though."

"You know that's never going to happen," I replied, while leaning up. "Boys live with women. Women live with men." "That's so out-dated," she stated, while rolling her eyes.

"Call it what you want to, but that's how I am," I stated, and then really looked at her. "And I don't wanna live with you anyway. I can't trust you. You shitted on me when I needed you, and now I'm home you think I'm a forget how you carried me? You better think again," I said, and stood before I let her have it with both barrels. She'd really carried me, and had the nerves to think that everything was going to go back to normal. Cut the jokes.

CHAPTER 4

LATOYA

It was a little after six when Kyle called. At the time, I was in the middle of getting ready for my dinner-date with Angie and Yolonda. Yolonda wanted to try out Calcius, this new restaurant-slash bar and grill that had opened downtown a few months ago because it had received good reviews in the paper. Since she was footing the bill, I was game.

"Hello," I said into the phone.

"Hey LaToya, it's Kyle," he said, though I already knew who it was. I'd memorized his number from the card, and not because I had plans on creeping with him either. When strange numbers appeared on my phone without first texting me and letting me know who they were it was a fifty-fifty chance I'd answer it.

"Hey Kyle, how are you?" I asked, while setting the eyeliner down so I could talk.

"Alright, and you?"

"Glad the weekend's here," I replied. "What plans do you have, or are you going to be working on some hot case?"

"Never is there rest for the deserving," he replied, and I knew he was telling the truth. Investigators at the Public Defender's Office very rarely had days off. "But the good thing is that in another eighteen months I'll be a lawyer so it'll all be worth it."

"That's good," I stated. "I didn't know you were planning on being a lawyer."

"From investigator to lawyer. From lawyer to Congressman, and from Congressman to President," he said, and chuckled.

"Big dreams," I playfully stated, though I was impressed.

"None bigger than hooking my First Lady," he said, and that got a smile out of me.

"Make sure she has enough money and influence to back you," I said, and laughed as he joined me.

"Not the reply I was looking for, but the truth nevertheless," he said. "So, what's your bank-account looking like?" he asked, and we again laughed together.

"Since money and power go hand in hand, definitely not good enough to help you become a lawyer."

"I've got that part, but since my bid for Presidency won't come for another twenty-years we'll worry about that when the time comes," he said, and I caught the use of the plural "we" instead of the singular "I," but left it alone. "Let's plan for the weekend."

"If you're working there's not much to plan for," I sensually stated.

"I am very good at doing two things at one time," he said. "See, I'm investigating this particular waitress at the Firehouse."

"Where's that at?"

"St. Albans," he replied. "And we could have dinner there while I observe her."

"Sorry, I'm going to Celsius with the girls tonight."

"Since girls is plural, I'm thinking three or four of them, which means I'm going to need to show up with a couple of guys," he said, and I let out one of those light-laughs that said, "no he didn't."

"Kyle."

"Hey, we're just stopping by to see if the hype is real or not," he said, and I knew he had to be smiling on the other end of the phone because it was in his tone.

CARLOS

As I pulled out from in front of my fathers, with K-Solo in the passenger-seat, we road in silence for a few minutes. We'd been with Pops for like two-in-a-half hours eating and clowning, and I was tired. Lisa last night and Scarlett this afternoon had me tired.

"So, what's up with you and Scarlett?" K-Solo asked, breaking the silence. "And no, you're not coming to live with me. Stay with Pops."

"I am," I said, agreeing with him. "I'm still trying to figure out what I'm a do though. You know I'm a need my own spot."

"Leave the streets alone for one," he said a hardedge to his tone, which caused me to cut my eyes to him. "I saw what you didn't see," he stated, while turning to look at me. "That crushed pops more than he let on."
"I know," I stated, while slightly nodding my head. "When he said he couldn't come back I knew it."

"So you know going back to the streets is going to crush 'em too, right?"

"What am I supposed to do then?" I asked. Hustling was really all I knew.

"I hollered at Uncle Dave and he said he'd get you a gig up at the Country Club until you found something else," he replied, and I was ready to tell him to beat it until it dawned on me that he was talking about The Country Club. Exclusive, for the rich, or those with enough influence to act like they were. The Edgewood Country Club.

"Let me think about it."

"Cool," he stated. "Now, let's get back to you and Scarlet. Did you tap it?"

"Did I," I replied, which caused him to laugh.

"I knew you were going back to her," he said. "I told you, you were fakin.'"

"We're not back together," I stated, cutting that short. "I'm cool on that."

"Better leave that pussy alone then," he said, and I was man enough to admit that he had a point there. "Did yah'll talk about the drama?"

"Shit went from whose crib is this to her bent over the couch with me diggin in 'err," I replied, shading the truth somewhat. Never was I telling him that she made me bust that quick. *Not in this lifetime.*

"You're going back," he said, with a knowing grin.

"Don't believe the hype," I stated, while shaking my head. "Never is she going to play me like that. I might just chew Tiffany's back out."

"I did," he stated, which caused me to bust out laughing, remembering him telling me how he dogged her out for not checking the drama before it got out of hand. He'd paid her a stack on the low for a night of how he wanted it fucking. Being thirsty, like she was, she took it and he dogged her out until he was tired and she was begging him to stop.

He used two-dildo and his joint on her the whole time, keeping all of her holes full. She finally paid him five-hundred dollars to stop once she realized that he had plans on doing it all night. He'd even come with K-Y Jelly and pussy lube for when she went dry.

"Matter a fact, I'm cool," I stated, and we laughed even harder.

LATOYA

Dinner had really been fun. About twenty-minutes into the meal, Kyle came in with two of his friends. It just so happened that a table right next to ours was open so they sat next to us. Of his two-friends, one was white and the other was black, and both were handsome... Add to that that Angie knew the black one, whose name was Varion, and within ten-minutes, we had a table for six.

Now we were at the bar, and me and Kyle were in one corner talking. Handing me my Strawberry Daqueri, he said, "see, that wasn't so bad."

"What?" I asked, though I knew what he was talking about.

"Hanging out with a white-guy," he replied, which made me grin and shake my head at the same time.

"Um, Kyle, I hang out with white-guys all of the time."

"That's work," he stated, while shaking his head. "You know what I mean."

"You chose good friends," I said, and looked from him to Angie and Varion talking, and then to Yolonda talking to the white-guy, whose name was Andy.

"Investigation," he stated, which caused me to look back at him with a raised eyebrow. "Varion was my ace in the hole."

"You knew he knew Angie, didn't you?" I asked, now catching on.

"Exactamundo," he replied, smiling. "Sure, hope you brought your dancing shoes."

"And I guess you can dance?" I asked. And you know I was looking at him with that look that said cut the jokes.

"I'm white, but I grew up in the Woo," he replied. The Woo was a rough black neighborhood on the West Side of Charleston which had its fair share of whites thrown in.

"That doesn't mean you can dance," I said, not buying it.

"Alright, we'll see," he said, and took a sip of his drink while I wondered why I hadn't left well enough alone. Did I really want to find out if he could dance?

CHAPTER 5

CARLOS

When Bra first told me about F.L.I.R.T.S, I was skeptical. For those of you who don't know F.L.I.R.T.S stands for Fat Ladies in Real Tight Skirts, and that's exactly what worked there. And they all wore tight skirts. To their credit, though they were all cute. But don't think that the only females that were up in there were fat chicks because you would've ended up looking stupid like I did when we rolled up in there. It was jam-packed with bad-women, most of which were anything but fat.

"And I guess you're going to walk pass and not speak," Somia said, and me, K-Solo, and Skeet pumped our breaks. I hadn't seen her when I looked over the crowd as I was coming in, but I was seeing her now. Before, she was a cutie, though on the slim side because she was into sports.

I guess she would've had an athletic-body because she had virtually no titties and a tight little butt, but that was back then. Baby girl was like that now to go along with her cute face she had the body to match. I guess having a baby really did wonders for some women.

"I'm definitely not walking pass any of yah'll and not speaking," I said, including her girls, Poo, Candy, and Ga'Milla in even though my words were just for her. And the look I gave her made sure that she knew it.

"When did you come home?" she asked, after we exchanged hellos with the rest of her girls.

27

"Yesterday," I replied. "And I'm feelin some type of way that I'm just now seein you."

"Boy if you don't cut it out," she said, though she couldn't mask the tint to her cheeks. We both knew that before I would've spoken and kept it moving, but now she definitely had my attention.

Taking my phone out I took her picture and handed her the phone and she put her number in without me saying anything. Yep, yah boy still had it.

"Don't get me caught-up in no beef with no dumb hoes," she said while handing me the phone back.

"I don't do drama," I said, and gave her a hug, said my good-byes and we were out.

"And they say the pussy's like that," K-Solo said, after we were out of hearing distance.

"Fire," Skeet chimed in, and added "and she goes both ways." With a knowing grin.

"Cool, cool," I said, while nodding my head. I didn't know when I was hitting that, but I knew I was going to get at her. Especially after what Skeet had just said.

LATOYA

When we came in the club, it was a few minutes till ten so the music wasn't blasted. That was good because I hated having to scream to be heard above the music.

"It's not all that packed," Angie said, as we walked side-by-side to the bar, while on the hunt for an empty table. And since I was wearing my blue-jean Miss Me outfit, with "Miss Me" imprinted on my butt, the back of the jacket, and my shirt, all in florescent-white, we were drawing our fair share of attention. And yes, all of my girls were dressed to impress as well. Yolanda did have on a pair of Red-Bottoms.

"Good," I stated, just as I felt Angie pull me.

"Come on girl, there's a table open," she said, while making a beeline for the table with me in tow.

CARLOS

"Is that LaToya from the East?" I asked K-Solo, as we leaned against the bar watching her and Angie abruptly turn from the isle and make their way towards an empty-table, with Yolanda, two-white dudes, and Varian bringing up the rear.

"None other," Skeet, my dude from the West, replied.

"And she's single," K-Solo said, and filled me in on the gossip about her situation. While listening to him I began formulating a plan on how I was going to get her. And I didn't just mean smash either. Baby girl was wifey-material.

LATOYA

At about eleven, the club was in full swing. It was so packed that if you left you might not get back in for another hour. I had been on the dance floor with my girls for a few songs now, and in the middle of dancing with some guy, I didn't know I looked over and saw Kyle dancing with a white-girl. Because the dance floor was so crowded, there wasn't much room between them so I couldn't tell if he could dance. With her butt pressed tightly to his private-area he looked like he could definitely get his grind on. After

29

dancing for four-straight songs, I needed a break. Thanking him, I turned and started making my way through the dancing-throng of people, but someone grabbed my arm and stopped me. Ready to tell whoever it was that I didn't want to dance anymore, I turned and saw it was Carlos and changed my mind. And this time I put my body all up against his.

CARLOS:

I was never gladder to be on a packed dance floor than now. Her body was so soft. And I'm talking about the front and the back. When we started out dancing we were face to face, and then she got white-girl close on me. One of my legs ended up between hers, and one of hers was between mines, with her breasts on my chest and we were getting it in. And she had to be feeling the effects because I had a chubby long before she turned around and backed that thang up on me. When she did that, the flagstaff went from half-mast to full just like that.

LATOYA

After about forty-five minutes, I knew Carlos needed a break before he ejaculated on himself. I also needed to cool my coochie off. Yes, I was moist.

"I'm tired. I need to sit down," I hollered into his ear

"Thank God," he hollered back, which made me smile. Taking my hand, he lead the way off the dance floor and to the table he was sitting at. Leaning over, until his mouth was right next my to ear, he said, "what are you drinking on?"

"A dirty martini, extra dry," I sensually purred into his ear.

"Keep playin with me and I'm a be back with yah jacket and we out," he said, with absolutely no hint of humor in his tone.

"So I take it you're not back with Scarlett?"

"I wouldn't be up in your face if I was," he replied, and that had a double meaning, which lead to implications I didn't like. "I'll be back with the drinks and we can finish this."

"Alright," I stated.

CARLOS:

As I headed towards the bar, I was looking for Bra and Skeet to let them know that it might be an early night for yah boy. I tried to holler at LaToya before I ended up with Scarlett, but I shut it down no, sooner than me and Scarlett were official. Now I was about to open it right back up. Not seeing them, I found a spot at the bar and ordered drinks, along with two Corona's. Handing the bartender my money, I turned to look around and see if I could find them when I saw Scarlett standing there with a white-chick that looked like she was every bit of six-feet tall. With legs that looked like they just kept on going. I couldn't tell if she had a butt, but if she did, it was more than likely small because she was on the slim side. But in the breasts department she was right.

"What's up," I said to Scarlett.

"You get on my nerves," she stated, mean mugging me and then storming off. It all happened so fast that both me and the white-girl were a bit taken aback as she stormed off.

Looking back at the white-girl, we both looked each other over. It was then that I noticed that she was wearing an all Gucci out-fit, with the matching bag in tow. Bad and paid, I said to myself as we again locked eyes and she smiled, turned and headed in the same direction that Scarlett had just stormed off in.

Taking my phone out I started to text K-solo a message, but the bartender interrupted me when she sat the drinks in front of me with the change. Motioning her to keep the change I hurriedly sent him a text letting him know that I was hollering at LaToya at the table, but I needed him to scoop the white-girl up that was with Scarlett for me and get her number.

Getting the drinks, I went back to the table and sat them down. Sitting down, I said, "I got you a Corona in case you were thirsty."

"Thank you," she stated, and reached for the Corona. Moving her chair over so that we wouldn't have to scream, she said "how long have you been home?"

"Yesterday," I replied, and picked up my shot of Rosay.

"I can tell," she said, and took a sip of her beer while boldly staring me in the eyes. And it took me a second to realize what she was talking about.

"What's up with them digits?" I asked, mainly because I was at a loss as to what to say to that.

"Is that all you want?" she asked.

Damn was all I could say to myself as I took a drink. Damn, and double-damn.

LATOYA:

When Skeet came, it was time for me to go. I didn't really like him, and I knew the feeling was mutual. Telling Carlos that I'd talk to him in a minute, I got my stuff together and went back to my table. While making my way back I wondered where this was going? I'd been as forward with him as I had ever been with a man. True, I did know him. We went to High School, and was friends of sorts. Though we had never done anything, he had taken me out a few times. And then right after we graduated Scarlett came along and he was off of the market.

He was a good man who knew how to treat a woman. I could tell that by the way he treated her. But, he was just now coming home so who knew what he wanted to do as far as a relationship went.

Arriving back at the table, glad to see that both Angie and Yolanda were there, I sat down and happily said, "guess who's going to be my new man?"

"What's his name?" Yolanda asked, the smile falling from her face.

"Kyle," Angie replied, and even my happy look vanished.

"Ewe, where do they do that at?" I asked, looking at them like they were on a bad trip.

"Might wanna tell him that then," Yolanda replied, and nodded her head in Angie's direction, who was sitting to my left, which was the direction that Kyle's table was at. And when I looked at him, I saw him snapping his fingers and bobbing his head to the music, while looking at me smiling. Guess he still wanted that dance.

CARLOS:

When K-Solo came to the table with the white-girl in tow, I heard Shake saying, "don't knock it until you try it." Standing, I told him I'd be back, grabbed her hand and took her to the back of the dance-floor where people were standing around leaning against the wall as they took a break. And where Scarlett wouldn't be at because she couldn't dance. Finding a spot against the wall, I pulled her into my arms so we could talk in each other's ear.

"Don't get me caught up in nothing," she said, which made me smile. She was telling me that she was game, but she didn't want to get caught up in any drama.

"Don't start none won't be none," I said. "What's up for the night?" I asked, and my hand lowered from the small of her back to her butt.

"When and where?" she replied. And to accentuate her point she took my ear lobe between her teeth and started sucking on it.

LATOYA

I don't know how it happened, but we ended up almost towards the back of the dance-floor, which was fine by me. Maybe it was me trying to get in the middle of everyone dancing so it wouldn't be that many people who saw me dancing with a white-guy, or maybe it was the good Lord wanting to show me something because, while we were dancing I saw Carlos and a white-girl all hugged up. At first, it looked like they were talking until she kissed him on the neck. And I knew it was a kiss when his hands lowered to her butt.

Oh well, I said to myself, trying to reason away the anger that was building within me. He wasn't my man so he wasn't really cheating on me. But he knew I wanted him, and he was choosing a white-girl over me. Now that really pissed me off Royally.

CARLOS

It was about thirty-minutes from closing time, and I was ready to go. Bra had left about forty-five minutes ago. The only reason I hadn't left with him was because LaToya had jive-like transformed on me, and I couldn't figure out why. And every time I tried to get her to step off to the side with me so I could find out what as up she told me to hold on and went back to talking to either her girls or the white-boy.

I finally grew tired of it and bounced. It was so many shorties trying to bless my game so I wasn't tripping. On top of that, I wasn't even certain she was going to bless me with some tonight so I was out. I was trying to creep with Melissa anyway. All I was waiting on was for her to hit me up and let me know she'd shook Scarlett and it was on. I'd find out what was up with LaToya tomorrow.

LATOYA:

Yes, I gave him the some-what cold shoulder. I wanted to tell him, but I didn't wanna look like I was being jealous over somebody that wasn't mines, so I kept my mouth shut. And when he finally left, I was a bit relieved.

Leaning over, Angie said, "what was that about?"

"Nothing," I replied, but my tone caused her to back-up some and look at me.

"Alright," she stated, but her tone, along with the look she gave me, let me know that this conversation was far from over.

"Are you ready to go?" I asked.

"Been ready," she replied, though the look on her face hadn't changed one bit. She knew something was up that I wasn't telling her.

CHAPTER 6

CARLOS:

Giving Skeet some dap, he hopped out of my ride and got in his. Waiting on him to pullout and lead the way out of the parking lot, I dialed Scarlett's number.

"Why?" was her opening statement when she answered the call.

"Why what?" I asked, not knowing what she was talking about. More less caring.

"Why did you disrespect me like that?"

"Why'd I disrespect you like what?" I asked, my tone matching her shitty one.

"Quit acting like you don't know what I'm talking about," she replied, her tone now one of exasperation.

"Have you been drinking?" I sarcastically asked.

"What's that have to do with anything?" she asked, just as my phone beeped to let me know that I had a text.

"Hold on," I replied.

"I bet you better not put me on hold."

"You wanna get hung up on?" I asked, tired of her nonsense.

"I bet you better not," she replied, and I hung up on her.

"She's lost in time," I said, and went to open the text.

"Where do you want me at, and when do I have to be there? Melissa," the text read, and my phone started ringing no, sooner than I was done reading it.

Sending Scarlett's call to voicemail, I sent Melissa a text back telling her to meet me at the Maudi Gra Casino in thirty-minutes, and I put my ride in drive and followed Skeet.

Hitting re-dial on Scarlett's missed-call, before the call could even get started she was calling me back. Taking the call, I said, "what's up?"

"Carlos, what's wrong?" she asked, her tone now drastically changed. If I didn't know any, better I'd say she was on the verge of crying.

"You," I replied. "How the fuck you gone act like you're my woman? Check me over another broad?"

"But you did it right in front of me after we spent the afternoon making love."

"Fuckin," I stated, correcting her misunderstanding of our afternoon activities. "And you knew the deal on that when I went to take a shower, so miss me with that," I barked.

"So, we're done just like that?" she asked, as I coasted to a top at the red light beside of Skeet.

"Scarlett, you left me the first month I was in the Regional. I'm a do me and you do you. Worry about gettin me my money before I move in yah spot," I replied, while wondering what she was tripping on.

"I said you could move in."

Cutting her off, I said, "that's not the type of moving in I was talking about. I'm talking about me moving in and you moving out," I stated, and then hung-up and sent K-Solo a text to let him know what I was on.

LATOYA

As soon as I pulled out Angie said, "alright, what happened? And don't try the nothing reply either, because I'm not buying it. At first, you're gushing about how he's the next Mr. Wonderful, and then you're giving him the cold-shoulder."

"Who, Carlos?" Yalonda asked.

"Yes," I replied, and then told them about seeing him with the white-girl in the back of the club all hugged up and kissing.

"Not Carlos," Yalonda said, and asked a couple of times for good measure.

"Why is it that they mess with white-girls?" Angie asked, and slightly shookher headin frustration.

"Before tonight I never knew he messed with them," I said, for some reason wanting to defend him.

"Like a sister isn't good enough for them," Angie stated, with a bit of an attitude in her tone. "But no sooner than we mess with a white-boy we're selling out."

"Sold out," Yalonda stated, as I pulled-off. "I'm young, single, and open to mingle. And the color of their skin is the last thing on my mind," she said. I don't know about Angie, but that was kind of like a revelation for me. I'd never known her to mess with white-men before.

"No, you didn't," Angie stated, while turning in her seat to look at Yolonda, who was in the back seat. I guess this was a revelation for her too.

"Girl, you do not broadcast you're messing with a white-man," she replied, while nodding her head. "Especially when

39

one of your really good friends is a full-fledged Black Panther."

"I am not," Angie stated, and I cracked-up laughing.

"Anyway, I don't mess with them in a relationship type of way," Yolonda said. "I don't see my parents being that understanding about me bringing one home for dinner. It's just more of having fun."

"You're better than me," Angie stated, and shook her head in disgust.

"No, I just have less drama than you," Yolonda said, which was true. Yolonda never had any relationship drama, while Angie on the other hand seemed to be involved in it in one form or another. "For me, it's not about love. It's about positioning myself for a better tomorrow. When Mr. Right comes along I'll worry about that then."

"What if he's white?" Angie asked. Now I'll be honest, I was curious about that answer myself.

"What if he's Mexican, Italian, or Creole?" Yolonda asked. "Or black and a dog?" she added.

"Would you choose the black-dog, or the white-guy?" I asked.

"I'd rather be dogged by my own than someone else's," Angie replied.

"That wasn't the question," I stated.

"Would you mess with a white-boy?" Angie asked me. "Would you mess with Ron?"

"I don't know," I honestly replied, which was a different answer than the one I would've given had the question been posed earlier. "But what I wouldn't do is date a dog simply because he was black. If that's the case I can do bad by myself."

"Amen to that," Yolonda stated.

CHAPTER 7

LATOYA:

After I dropped, everybody off our conversation was still on my mind. Would I call a white man my man? That was deep. True, the thought of it kind of sent a shudder through me, but Yolanda did make a lot of sense. So much, sense that she had changed my perspective on the issue somewhat. Not enough for me to take Kyle up on his offer of being his First Lady, but somewhat. With Kyle on my mind, I dialed his number. I might as well have someone to talk to on my ride home.

"Have you made it home yet?" he asked when he answered the call, with the sound of "Bad and Boujie" playing in the background.

"No, I'm on my way though," I replied, while smiling. He was listening to that while thinking of me.

"Where are you at?"

"Passing the Kroger's by Valley Bell," I replied, which was on the West Side of Charleston where both Angie and Yolanda lived.

"Meet me at Hardees."

"No thank you," I sweetly replied. "I can make a breakfast sandwich a lot quicker than I'll get one in that long line."

"Is that an invitation for a night-cap?" he asked.

42

"Sorry Kyle, I don't do nightcaps," I replied, my tone still sweet. "Night-caps lead to things happening that wouldn't have happened had alcohol not been present."

"Night-caps don't always lead to people sleeping together," he said, and that sounded so lame that I had to laugh.

"Kyle, if you don't cut the jokes," I said, and he ended up laughing with me.

"Don't fault me for trying," he good-naturedly stated.

"I won't," I said.

"So, is there a convenient place I need to be at tomorrow so we can hang out?"

"My place at six for dinner," I replied. Yes, that even surprised me. That definitely wasn't what I had intended to say. Seriously.

"Bowling afterwards?" he asked, which made me wonder how he knew that I liked to bowl until I remembered that it was in the bio on my page.

"Can you bowl?"

"Can a duck float?" he replied, as if my question offended him.

"I'll call and reserve us a lane," I said, and added "don't get over there and get embarrassed."

"I don't know the meaning of the word," he said, and I smiled. He must really be able to bowl, I said to myself, now glad that I had made the date. It might be fun after all.

CARLOS

When I pulled into the parking lot and finally found somewhere close to park, I left the car running while I sent Melissa a text to let her know that I was here. After that, I sent LaToya a text to make sure that she made it home alright, and asked her what went wrong?

"Room 411," Melissa's reply text said, and I grinned. Her treat for my meat, I said as I turned the car off. I might just give her the whole business, I was thinking as LaToya texted me back.

"You forgot to tell me you had a boo," it read.

Ready to call her, I remembered Melissa was waiting on me inside and checked that idea. The last thing I needed right now was for her to say come to her spot, so I texted back, "I don't."

"Sure, looked like it the way the two of you were hugged-up, or do you routinely hug and kiss white-girls?" she hit right back.

She saw me with Melissa. "Shit," I stated, and looked towards the hotel and then back to the phone, debating on what to do. "Give me five and I'm calling. That was nothing." I text back.

"Call me tomorrow. I'm getting ready for bed."

"Cool. Good night," I texted back, and locked my car up and headed for the hotel. Tomorrow would take care of tomorrow. Tonight, I was about to put my hard-hat on and get to work.

Going in the hotel, I went to the elevators and took one up to the fourth-floor. Going down to room 411, I saw that it had a "Do Not Disturb" sign on the door, but knocked anyway. That was for everybody but me. I was here to work, and the sign was there to make sure that nobody got in the way.

"Hold on," I heard Melissa say from the other side of the door, and then the peephole darkened for a second. Opening the door, she said, "took you long enough," and my witty reply got stuck on the tip of my tongue. She stood there in a sheer white-lace Victoria Secret's teddy, along with the matching garter-belt and gown.

And when I say sheer I was seeing it. Even the tattoo of the bouquet of roses that started from her pelvic-area and came up and spread out across her flat-stomach and went all of the way up to the bottom of her breast. There, the tattoo continued between them, and on either side, stopping partway up.

Getting my mojo back, ready to say something slick, I instead went in, shut the door and backed her up against the wall. She was like two-inches taller than me, barefooted, but that was cool with me. "How do you take it off?" I asked, looking down at the teddy.

"You don't like it?" she purred.

"Love it, but it's going to get in the way so we might as well take it off," I replied, and looked from it to her long blond hair that went most of the way down her back. "Are you a natural blond?"

"Yes," she replied, and watched as I lifted my hand to feel her breast.

"I thought they were fake earlier," I said, feeling the side of her breast.

"All naturale," she stated, and then cupped my cheeks in her hand and lightly kissed me.

Now I was in-between a rock and a hard-place here. See, I didn't kiss jump-offs because I didn't know where their mouths had been. I didn't even kiss Scarlett when I twisted her back out earlier, though I did play sucky-face with Lisa. She had mistress status. Fuck it, I said to myself, and brushed my lips against hers. Her breath did smell like she'd just finished brushing her teeth, and I had alcohol on mines. And we all know that alcohol kills everything. When I gently squeezed her breast she moaned, and I deepened the kiss as her nipple hardened beneath my hands. Now, you know I was doing some comparisons.

With this being, the first white-chick I'd ever been with I was comparing her kisses to blacks, as well as the feel of her skin and all of that. She got a bonus for her aggressiveness, as well as getting the room. I wasn't all the way feeling her holding my cheeks like that, but she could kiss. Me, I wasn't all that good at it, but she could get it in. After unzipping the teddy to free her breasts I lost interest in it and focused totally on the kiss.

We were tonguing and everything, and like every ten or fifteen seconds, she would moan into my mouth, which had me all the way amped. Shit, she had me feeling like my kissing game was like that. Breaking the kiss, she said "back up some." Taking a step back, she dropped to a squatting position in front of me and unbuckled my belt. Seeing that she was about to free Moby, I figured it was time to pop the hood on the trunk, so I took my shirt off just as she was unbuttoning my pants.

Now I never got around to telling you what was under the hood. See, for twenty-months I spent two-hours a day, five-days a week, getting it in. From lifting weights to Navy Seals, I got it in. And add thirty-minutes of running three or four days a week and you can understand that by the time my shirt hit the floor she was looking at my chest within that ole' my God look.

"Oh baby," she cooed, while raising back up to a standing position, totally forgetting about freeing Moby, as her eyes roamed from my chest, abs, and traps. Running her hands over my upper-body that wasn't enough for her so she leaned down and started kissing my chest until I busted out laughing.

"What's so funny?" she asked, as she leaned up and moved her hair out of the way.

"You're tall as shit," I replied. Her bending over like that looked crazy as hell.

"And you're beautiful," she stated, and kissed me on one side of my chest and then the other, and then leaned back up. "I can't wait to get you in bed."

"Shit, what are we waitin' for?" I asked, and turned the dead bolt.

"You," she replied, while smiling.

"Let me get these off," I said, and finished taking my pants off, while she crossed her arms and watched. "You can finish undressing right here if you want."

"Okay," she stated, and took her time taking the teddy off. Finishing by turning around and bending over she pushed it down over her knees so I could get a birds-eye view of that pussy. And you can believe yah boy had a nice view of it too. She had one of those skinny-girl gaps, and that peach-pit was right there poking out for me to see.

"That's what I'm talking about right there," I said, as she leaned back up and turned to face me. Her breasts were sitting up super-pretty with absolutely no hang-time. They definitely made up for her lack of a butt, because she didn't have any of that. And that wasn't a fair representative of the white-girls in Charleston either. There's quite a few that'll make you think they've got black in their blood that thing back there is so right.

"You like?" she asked, lifting her arms out to the side and slowly turning in a full circle.

"Do I," I replied, halfway through her turn.

"Good," she stated, and turned to face me. "Good," she again said, and paused as a mischievous smile creased her lips, "because I like him too," she said and then reached out and took a hold of Moby.

"Show me," I said.

"Your wish is my command," she stated, and lead the way to the bedroom, where she sat down on the bed and proceeded to lavish Moby with so much attention that, by the time she was halfway through, I would have sworn she was in love with him.

CHAPTER 8

CARLOS:

Okay, so you're mad I didn't give you the details of everything that happened, but blame the editor. This is a tasteful-story, not a debauching one, and I went past Zanesville last night. But for the freaks out there, let's just say we got it in. Tossing salads, and singing ballads style. After about five-minutes of comparison I gave up on it and accepted the fact that she was a woman, and like any other, I was leaving a lasting impression on her. One that had me laid out until one-thirty the next day.

I guess she left one on me too. Surfacing into consciousness, I blinked a few times to clear my vision. Now I'll be honest, I was so tired afterwards that I didn't have the strength to get in the shower, but I made myself get under the water long enough to brush my teeth and wash her fluids off of me. When she had an orgasm, she shot it everywhere

It took a few seconds for me to catch on that I was in bed alone. Once that sunk in, I sat up and looked around the room, wondering where she was at. The first thing that caught my attention was my clothes folded up, with a note on top of it, sitting on the chair beside of the bed. Scooting over, I grabbed the note and read,

"Thank you for a wonderful night. I wanted to wake you before leaving, but you looked delightfully exhausted so I reluctantly left you asleep. I booked the room for the rest of the day so doesn't be in a rush to leave. Who knows, you may be up for a repeat performance tonight. You know how to reach me. Tah, tah."

"I can't wait to talk to Shake," I groggily said, while setting the note down and getting my phone. I needed to hit Solo and Pops and let them know I was alright, as well as check my messages. After taking care of that, I ordered breakfast from room services, and went to take a real shower. And when I was done with that, I was calling LaToya.

LATOYA:

If I didn't have plans for Saturday-afternoon, I cleaned the house, which is what I was doing when Carlos called. "Hello," I said, kind of out of breath.

"What are you into that has you out of breath?" he playfully asked.

"Cleaning house," I replied.

"The way you sound, you need a break, so cop a squat," he said, his tone still playful.

"I do not sound that bad," I said, smiling.

"Didn't you run track in high school?"

"And played tennis," I replied, though I'd never made the team. I'd never made it any further than the practice-team.

"Do you still work out?"

"Not since I graduated," I sheepishly replied. I'd stopped working out in college because I didn't run track.

"Might wanna consider working out with me."

"I will," I said. Who knew where we were going, and if it ended up being in the right direction then I would gladly try working out if for no other reason than to spend more time with him.

"Cool, now about last night. Can I come up in half an hour?" he asked, and I looked at the clock. It was a quarter till three, which meant that he would get here around three-thirty. And with Kyle coming at six, I needed to start dinner no later than four-thirty. If he came over I'd have to start with him here, And that wasn't happening, I said to myself.

"I have stuff everywhere, and by the time I get it back together it's going to be time to shower and go over Angie's. She's cooking tonight," I replied, artfully lying.

"I was hoping you were, and was thinking about inviting me over."

"And if I was, what would you want me to cook?"

"What you like, though I'm more concerned with what you cooked it in," he replied, and there for a second I was speechless. "You, cooking in a burgundy Teddy, with the matching bow and pumps, sounds good to me."

"And what would you be wearing while I'm doing this?" I sensually asked, setting him up for the spoiler.

"Matching Polo boxers, with some Timbo's on," he replied, and I cracked up laughing. I must admit that was the last reply I was expecting.

"I wasn't expecting that," I admitted.

"You thought I was going to say naked, didn't you?"

"No, I just didn't think you'd say that," I replied, and paused. "Where's the white-girl going to be at while all of this is happening?" I asked, springing the spoiler.

"The same place your white-boy's going to be. About their business," he replied, and laughed.

"What white-boy?"

"The one whose face you were all up in while you were stuntin' over nothing last night."

"Over nothing? I don't consider you hugging and kissing another woman nothing," I said, and added, "especially a white one."

"Do I have a lock on the pussy?" he asked, his tone now serious.

"No," I replied, after a slight-pause and enough hesitation to let him know that it could happen if he acted right.

"And you don't have a lock on the dick," he said. "What you saw really wasn't nothing, but if you're tryin' to put a lock on the dick you need to let me know."

"How do I?" I asked. His straight-forwardness kind of had me open.

"Let me know when you come back from Angie's and we can either chill at your spot for the night, or hit the Casino."

"I'll call you when I come back," I replied. Damn, and just like that I'd agreed to spend the night with him. If that was, what it took to put a lock on it then so be it.

CARLOS:

"There has to be a reason why you're blowing me up," I said into the phone, after having spent the last ten-minutes sending Scarlett's calls to voice-mail. On top of that, I had been ignoring her texts for the last two-hours.

"Why are you ignoring me?" she asked, pissed.

"Because I want too," I replied, while starting the car. "Now, what do you want?"

"Do you want your funky ass money back?" she asked, and that quickly perked me up. That was twenty-k she was talking about.

"Scarlett, find something else to play about," I replied. Outside of K-Solo and Pops looking out for me I was on busted status, with no come-ups in the immediate future.

"I'm at the house. I'll be here until six," she said, and hung-up on me, and twenty-minutes later I was parking in front of her house. I wasn't doing any playing about my money.

As I was walking up the sidewalk, the door opened and I saw Scarlett standing slightly behind the door in a white terry-cloth robe. "I figured if I said something about your money you'd break your neck getting here," she sarcastically stated.

CHAPTER 9

LATOYA

I must admit dinner with Kyle was nice. And he was a perfect guest, even helping put the leftovers up and wash the dishes. By the time, we were done with everything it was fifteen after eight and we had to go. I had reserved the lane from nine to midnight, and we had to be there fifteen-minutes early.

"I'm confused about something," he said, while opening the passenger-door of his 2012 Range Rover so I could get in.

"What's that?" I asked, stopping from getting in to look at him.

"You don't have a bowling ball or shoes, but you say you can bowl. Why am I not convinced?" he asked, with a smirk.

"I do, but I only use them for the bowling league," I replied.

"Bowling league?" he asked, with a raised-eyebrow.

"Yes, I bowl with the Clerk's team," I sweetly replied, and the smile vanished from his face. "I'll use what they have at the alley, if it's alright with you?"

"You tricked me," he replied, and I blew him a kiss and got in and he shut the door behind me. Coming around and getting behind the wheel, he said, "you know you tricked me, right?" while putting the keys in the ignition.

"Didn't you tell me you could bowl?" I sweetly asked.

"Just because I can play ball doesn't mean I can make State's team," he replied, and I laughed.

"You were going to smear me all over the alley, wasn't you?" he asked, and started the truck up.

"I would've taken it easy on you once I realized you couldn't bowl," I replied, while still laughing.

"Do you like baseball?" he asked, and smiled. "You do know the Powers game just started, right?"

"Yes, but I didn't dress for it," I replied. "By the time, I got ready for the game it would be over. Don't worry," I said, and patted him on the arm, "it'll be fun."

"I didn't know getting the breaks beat off you was fun," he jokingly stated.

CARLOS:

As Pops came back in the living room and sat down, I said,

"Pops, I've got a problem."

"Talk to me," he stated, while setting his glass on the coaster on the coffee table.

"I have a white and black woman, and we all live in the same house," I said, and that caused him to go bug-eyed on me.

"Get out of here!" he exclaimed.

"Straight talk," I replied, while looking at him funny. Pops was a smooth dude and I think that was the first time I saw him get excited like that.

"You just came home yesterday. How'd you pull that off so quick?" he asked, regaining his cool.

Telling him the edited story about Melissa and Scarlett, I said, "she sprung it on me this afternoon."

"That's deep," he stated, and I knew, because of Scarlett, he wasn't feeling it.

"It's even deeper than that," I said, and paused for a second.

"There's this shorty named LaToya."

"I thought you were talking to Lisa?"

"Crushin' partners," I replied, while grinning and slightly shaking my head.

"You know son," he said, and paused. Now, when he hit me with "son" I knew he was serious and was about to drop some serious game so I always paid close attention to what he had to say. "A woman will say what she has to say to get what she wants, or put herself in a position to get it. A crushing partner doesn't do what she did for you. That's a woman with her eyes dead-set on a man. And that's a woman you shouldn't just cast to the wind either. She's shown you she'll ride the river with you," he said.

And, I'll be honest, I hadn't really thought about it like that. I mean, the only conversations me and Lisa had were about her putting it on me when I came home, or just everyday conversation. We'd never talked about being in a relationship together. "Your two-women are cool, though you're a fool for getting anywhere near Scarlett. But choose wisely. You could be choosing the mother of your children."

LATOYA:

Seeing that the call was from Angie, I said, "it's Angie. I have to take it." She knew I was on a date, and I knew she wouldn't be calling unless it was important.

"Alright," Kyle stated, as he turned on to the Boulevard, which was a straight-shot to the bowling alley.

"What's up girl?" I said, into the phone.

"Girl, you are not going to believe this," she said, and I wondered what was going on now? By the way, she was sounding, it had to be serious because she was hyped. "Scarlett just put a picture up on Instagram and Facebook of her and Carlos in bed. And she's talking about she's got her man back," she stated, and I exhaled in a rush of breath as my eyes got glassy.

"I'll call you back later," I stated, and hung-up. *God, what did I ever do to deserve this*, I thought while switching to text-mode and sending Carlos a blistering text.

CARLOS:

"Why did I have to hear you and Scarlett were an item again on Instagram? You're a dog and an ass," the text from LaToya read, causing me to close my eyes and groan.

"That bad?" Pops asked.

"LaToya found out I was back with Scarlett because the idiot put pictures up on Instagram," I replied. And I knew what pictures they were to. Her laying on top of me, with the sheet high-enough to cover her butt. Just exposing her bareback and the side of her face and mines.

"The most devious creature God created was a woman," Pops said, and busted out laughing.

"It's not what it seems. I'm with you like I said," I texted back, mainly because I was mad at Scarlett.

"Lose my number," was her reply, and I flopped back on the couch and closed my eyes.

"I take it damage control didn't work," Pops said, with a bit of sympathy in his tone.

"Have you ever felt like life was going way too fast?"

Nodding his head in reply, he said, "you just came home yesterday. Slow it down. You left with women problems. Don't come home to them."

"True," I stated, and sat there for a few seconds just looking at the ceiling, while gathering my thoughts. Sending Lisa a text telling her that I needed her, I then started mentally wrestling with what I was going to do with Scarlett. I knew once Lisa found out she'd be mad, though she'd try and hide it. But I wasn't feeling what Scarlett had done. I really did have plans on telling both LaToya and Lisa. It wasn't right that they had found out like that though. I wasn't feeling that. And I wasn't leaving my newfound family either. At least not yet anyway. Boy, what a dilemma.

CHAPTER 10

LATOYA:

The first game I bowled with a vengeance. I was so mad at Carlos that I forgot I was supposed to take it easy on Kyle. By the end of the fifth-frame, the game was all but over.

"Well, let's see," Kyle said, while looking up at the score on the over-head screen. "I'd say you got to feeling bad around the seventh-frame and turned it down on me."

"Sixth," I sheepishly replied. I'd bowled four-strikes and a spare the first five-frames.

"And I didn't even with after that. I suck," he said, and smiled and I affectionately nudged him with my shoulder.

"Practice makes perfect," I stated, and stood.

"It's ten-after ten and I suck. By midnight this'll be a crime scene."

Smiling, I said, "why don't you try plying me with alcohol and see if that works. Who knows, you may come away in one piece."

"That sounds like a good idea," he said, while standing.

"Get some pistachio's too," I said.

Nodding his head, he said, "be right back," and headed towards the restaurant while I went to get a ball to take some more frustration out on the pins. Every pin looked just like Carlos.

CARLOS:

On my way downtown, Scarlett called and I was thinking about sending the call to voice-mail, but changed my mind. "What?" I asked.

"I've been calling you for the last past two-hours. Where have you been that you couldn't take my call?" she asked, put out.

"With Pops," I replied.

"How is he doing?" she asked, her tone now totally changed. She now had a bit of hesitation in it.

"Wondering what I'm trippin' on."

"Did you tell him we're back together," she replied, and I was tempted to tell her yes, as well as his thoughts about it, but changed my mind.

"I'm not trying to get put out and told never to come back," I sarcastically replied.

"Why would he do that for?" she asked, and I busted out laughing. "I don't find anything funny either."

"I can't believe you asked that stupid-ass question," I replied. "After all the slimy shit you did, you know why he can't stand you."

"That really hurt," she said, in a low-tone.

"Hold on," I said, as I passed through the green light at five-corners and my phone beeped. Seeing that it was Lisa calling, I clicked over and said, "you get my message?"

"I just saw it. Are you alright?" she worriedly asked in a rush of breath.

"What time do you get off?" I asked, and added, "I'm alright though. I really am."

"Really?" she asked, her concern riding heavy in her voice. "And don't lie to me either."

"I'm cool. Straight up," I replied. "What time are you getting off?"

"I'm off now, but I'm helping clean up."

"What are you on for the night? Can I spend the night?"

"Yes," she replied. "Are you coming to pick me up?"

"I'm about to get on the interstate now."

"Call me when you're out front," she said, and we exchanged good-byes and I hung up.

Clicking over, I said, "are you still there?"

"Yes."

"My fault for keeping you on hold for so long, but your picture has me doing some damage control."

"What damage is there to control? We're back together and that's that," she smartly stated.

"True, true," I replied, not even bothering to waste my breath explaining to her that was something I should've told them, not Instagram or Facebook.

"So, what time are you coming home?"

"About midnight," I replied. She thought home was her house, but after tonight, she'd learn where home really was. "It might be later, depending on what we get into."

"You could've went out with us."

"I'm cool," I stated, not wanting to open that door. Yeah it would be cool to be out with two women, but since one of them was her, it wouldn't be all that fun. "Where are you going too?"

"Nowhere now," she disappointedly replied. "I thought we were spending the evening with you."

"We'll see what's up tomorrow."

"What about tonight? You are coming home?" she inquisitively asked.

Smiling, I said, "I already told you I was, so chill with that."

CARLOS:

After a brief-kiss, and some light conversation, we road in silence to the interstate on McCorkle Avenue until we road past a darkened Laidly Field. It was then that Lisa broke the silence and asked the question I'd been waiting on.

"Are you back with Scarlett?"

"What do you think?" I asked, while glancing at her and then back to the road.

"Carlos, I saw the pictures so you don't have to lie to me," she replied, her tone letting me know that she was slightly put out.

"You didn't ask me if I twisted her back out, you asked if I was back with her," I stated, a grin now playing at the corners of my lips.

"Right," she stated, while slightly nodding her head, and then stopped. "You're not back with her, are you?" she asked, now putting everything together. "If you were you wouldn't be spending the night with me," she said, smiling.

"I knew you'd catch on," I said, while slightly nodding my head.

"What are you doing?" she asked, and the question kind of caught me off guard.

"What do you mean?" I asked. And I didn't have a clue what she meant either.

"You know what I mean," she replied, and I was ready to tell her that I didn't but she continued before I could say anything. "Why are you even messing with her after she left you like that?"

"Honestly, I've been a sucka for some good pussy for so long it's crazy," I jokingly replied. "But I'm not back with her like she thinks I am."

"She sent me a picture," she said, and picked up her phone and tapped the screen a few times, so I could see the picture. Glancing at it, I saw it was one of the pictures Scarlett had posted. The only difference was the message attached to it. It read, "Thx for keepin' him company but he's back home now."

"Wanna set the record straight?" I asked, while looking back to the road.

"What, that you're mines?"

"I didn't know that's what you wanted."

"I never knew it was an option," she replied, and added, "is it?" I wanted to say yes. I honestly did. Like Pops had said, she'd stood by me when I needed her, and all she'd asked was for my friendship. But it wasn't in me to do right, and she was the last person I wanted to wrong.

"Be honest with me," she stated, and added. "I at least deserve that."

"You deserve everything," I said and paused. "I can never shit on you, and that's what I'd be doing if I told you it was going to be me and you. Right now, it's not in me to do right, you feel me?"

"In a strange way I do," she replied, and nodded her head.

"But that's my pussy, don't get it twisted," I jokingly stated, though I was dead serious.

Smiling, she said, "you can have it when the ding-ding's mine. But what are you going to do bout Scarlett?"

"Enjoy the show for as long as it lasts," I replied, and debated on telling her about Melissa. "But after you send her this picture setting the record straight it might be a wrap for a beautiful thing."

"What beautiful thing?" she asked, and her tone conveyed her displeasure at whatever my answer was to be.

"It's not just me and Scarlett. It's me, her, and this chick named Melissa. And we're one big family," I replied, and told her the edited story of how all of it happened. Maybe in hearing the story she'd understand the dilemma I was in. I mean, this was every man's dream. Two women at home, all my own.

LATOYA:

Bowling had been fun, as had the midnight meal of hamburgers and fries we'd shared. We didn't talk about work, just about each other. What we wanted out of life, as well as our partners. We didn't talk about bowling either. By the end of the second game, it was obvious I wasn't bowling so we went to the pool-hall and shot pool and played pinball. Both of which he trashed me at.

Now we were riding back to my place, and my mind was on Carlos. I couldn't understand why he'd done what he did. Not thinking, I audibly exhaled, while looking out over the Kanawha River as we road down the Boulevard.

"I didn't think tonight was that bad," he said, drawing me from my thoughts.

"Huh?" I asked, while turning to look at him.

Repeating what he said, he then said, "this has to be deep. Share it."

"Have you ever felt like life wasn't fair?" I asked, caught up in my own misery and not understanding the ramifications of the question.

"Definitely," he replied. "Every time I try talking to a sistah I feel it."

"Then why do you keep trying?"

"I'm single, looking for Mrs. Right, and not concerned about what color she is," he replied, adding a shrug of a shoulder. "It's just that every time I try color's always an issue. What's your gripe?" He asked, while looking back to the road.

"Men," I replied.

"Woe now. You can't lump us all together. You wouldn't wanna live in the shadow of my ex, and I'm definitely not trying to live in the shadow of yours," he said, which made sense. "At least let me kill myself on my own. I mean, I've already got one strike against me."

"What's that for?" I asked, without thinking.

"I'm white," he replied, and there was nothing I could say to that. No matter how I sugar coated it that was the reality of the situation right there.

"Does it bother you?"

"Does racism bother you?"

"Yes," I replied. I'd yet to meet a black person who wasn't bothered by it. "But it's not racism."

"Pray tell, what is it?" he jokingly asked.

"Peer-pressure," I replied, which is what it was for me. "If it was racism you'd know it. It's just the awkwardness of the situation, and everything that comes with it."

After a few seconds of silence, he said, "so, is that the nice way of telling me the most we're going to be is friends?"

"Right now, that's what I need," I replied, being honest with him. "Don't forget I just broke up with my man two-days ago. I can't just come out of one relationship and jump right into another one. I need time to get Michael out of my system," I said. I know, I would of been more than willing to jump into one with Carlos, but Kyle wasn't Carlos.

"Mind if I hang around and help?"

"I do need a date for the baseball game tomorrow night. And I specifically remember you telling me you needed a date so you could check out this waitress."

Smiling, he said, "that I do," and then paused, before adding, "and LaToya you're not slick either."

"Slick how?" I innocently asked.

"You also need time to see if you can handle the peer-pressure of going out with a white-guy."

Not saying anything for a few-seconds, I finally smiled and said, "that too," and we both shared a good laugh. I was human, and I cared about what those who cared about me thought about me. I wasn't a follower by any sense of the word, but I wasn't that type of leader either. But we'll see. Who knows what the future would hold.

* THE END *

Jody

Jody
CHAPTER 1

THE WOO 1990

Coming home from school, and tossing his book-bag on the couch Fish went to the kitchen to get a glass of the sweet lemon-lime Kool-Aid that his mother, Bev, had made last night for dinner. With them being the only, two living in the two-bedroom row-house apartment on Lippert-Street, he knew that there was still some left because he was the only one that drank it. She preferred her Pepsi, which she kept by the two-liters.

Coming down the steps and seeing his book-bag on the couch, Pat said "boy, how many times have I told you about leaving your book-bag on my couch? You know you need to take that up to your room."

"I'm getting' a glass of this 'aid and I'm on my way," he replied, while taking a glass from the cup-holder beside of the sink with one hand and opening the refrigerator with the other.

"Boy, you can't game a gamer," she said, coming around the couch and heading to the kitchen.

"Cut it out woman," he affectionately stated, as he reached for the of Kool-Aid.

"Dionne called. She said she needs you to call her back," she said, as she came through the small living room into the kitchen.

"She'll be alright," he said, while pouring the Kool-Aid into the glass.

As he turned she let the look of displeasure fall away to be replaced by her easy-grin. At sixteen, he was a spitting image of his father, who was one of the finest men in Charleston during his time. And just like his father, he styled himself as a mack. Though he thought he was slick, she knew. Women like Dionne, who were two and three-years older than him, were feigning for her baby. She'd told him on more than one occasion to use his head, but she had long-sense accepted the realization of which of his two heads were making the decision.

"What's up momma?" he asked, seeing her facial expressions shift, but not knowing why.

"Be here between seven-thirty and eight," she replied, and looked his five-foot eight-inch slim frame over. "And stay out of trouble."

"Don't I always?" he asked, and smiled before taking a drink.

"What plans do you have for the weekend?"

"Ahhh," he stated, once he came up for air. "You did this momma," he said, tipping the glass towards her. "I'm a need some money tomorrow so I can hang out at the mall and hit the midnights."

"Who are you going to the movies with?" she playfully asked, already knowing the answer.

"Date?" he asked, smiling. "Momma, you know I don't do no datin'," he said, and took another drink. Not only did he not date, the most attractive women to him were the

2

ones that had a man. He messed with single women, but as soon as they became too attracted and started to get designs on him, he was gone.

"You can't screw everything boy," she said, and saw him choke and almost spit the Kool-Aid all over the place.

Barely getting the Kool-Aid down without spitting it back out, Fish said "momma, you're trippin," and then laughed.

"Ain't nothin' new under the sun boy," she said. "Like father like son."

"My old dude call?" Fish asked, mainly because he wanted to change the subject.

"No," she replied. "Why don't you go and see him?"

"A new movie came out. It's gone be live at the midnights," he replied, killing that idea before it grew wings. He wasn't getting stuck in Montgomery for the weekend. At least not this one. He had a lot planned, beginning with a creep no sooner than he escaped his mother's clutches.

CHAPTER 2

Leaving out of his back door, Fish went up the steps and came out between the two apartment buildings on to Hutchinson Street. Turning right he walked down the sidewalk while looking across the street to see if Ebony had the door open to her apartment, which was her signal that her mother and brother wouldn't be home, and that it was on. Seeing that the door was open, he started to walk across the street, angling so that he would reach the other side of the street at the end of the block, when he saw her come to the front door and shut it.

Going around to the back of the building, he walked part-ways down the sidewalk that went the length of the ten-apartment row-house building until he came to her apartment and saw that the back door was open. Going up to the screen-door he saw her standing back some in the darkened kitchen in a black robe and opened the door.

Waiting until Fish shut the door, Ebony untied the sash on her robe and said, "did I do what you asked daddy?" she asked, and parted it some to reveal her nakedness with absolutely no shyness. True, this was the first time that Fish had seen her naked before, but she knew that her body was like that. On top of that, she knew that she was beautiful.

At five-foot six, dark-brown-skinned, with black-hair that fell to just below her shoulders, and a face that ensured that all of the street-hustlers competed for her favors by showering gifts upon her, she'd stopped being shy two years ago when she was fifteen. She knew that her boldness gave her power that a shy a girl didn't have. Power that she used to her fullest.

Letting his eyes travel over her nakedness while his fingers turned the bolt on the door, Fish's gaze paused at her trimmed black triangle. He knew that the pointer pointed in the direction that he wanted to go. The one that would make this a most enjoyable afternoon.

"Are you just going to stand there and stare?" she sensually asked, and opened the rope wider to show him more of her nakedness. She wasn't worried about being seen by anyone outside. She'd pulled the living-room blinds as well as the kitchen curtains, so the only eyes that would feast upon her loveliness was his.

"Nah," Fish replied, and went to her and took the ends of the robe and helped her out of it. Though he wasn't nervous or anything, her boldness was throwing him a bit. "How long we got?" he asked, as she turned and he saw her little onion and reached down to trail his fingers across it.

Pausing in her turning, she let his hand come to rest on her butt. She loved to be touched, and wanted him to touch her. That was something her man, didn't do a lot of which was why she was here with Fish. Moe just wanted to do it. He didn't want to pay Kitty the attention she deserved, nor really engage in much of any foreplay. Foreplay to him was kissing.

Once the clothes were off, he was all about getting up inside of her. The only good thing about him was that he had stamina so she always reached her climax. But after hearing, some of her girls talk about how good Fish was she wanted to experience it herself. If his attention to detail was even half as good as they said it was then this would be a regular occurrence for the two of them, and Moe would have to find him someone else.

"They won't be home until later," she finally said, and flexed her cheeks so they moved in his hand. "Do you like?" she asked, looking over her shoulder at him.

"Yeah," he replied, and let the robe fall to the floor while massaging her butt. It was nice and tight and the skin was super-soft. Putting his hand on the small of her back he said, "bend over," and gently put pressure on her back.

Turning some so that she would be able to rest both hands on the seat of the chair, Ebony waited until he was standing behind her again before bending over. She knew that he wasn't going to try to sex her because he still had his clothes on. Had he been naked she would never have bent over like this. She was here to be pleasured. Had she wanted someone to bounce all up inside of her she would have went to a hotel with Moe for the weekend.

As she bent over Fish trailed his finger down the seam of her butt-crack. Though to her she was probably thinking that he just wanted to touch her, which was influencing her because her breathing had quickened some, but he was, really, doing was making sure that nothing back there smelled fishy. As his finger passed across her anus, he slowed some.

He wanted to make sure that her butt didn't stink, so he would want to smell that finger too because he had plans on giving her the royal treatment. She was way too bad not to get it. As his finger passed over her anus, he quickly switched fingers and moved the new one across her slit, feeling her heat coming from her opening. "Touch me," she said in a low-voice, and moved her backside up some because she wanted his finger on her pleasure spot.

"How you want me to do it?" he asked, moving his finger to her opening and trailing it around it. She was hot and ready for him, he said to himself. He could feel her moisture on the tip of his finger.

"You know how," she replied, and moved back on his finger.

Letting it slide inside of her, he let it go in up to the knuckle, marveling at her tightness. The way she was tossing it at him, he would have thought that it would be looser, but it wasn't.

"Right there," she stated, and wiggled her behind around in a semi-circle. "Hmm," she moaned.

"I see you're ready for me," he said, and slowly took his finger out of her.

"No," she stated, wanting it back inside of her.

"Calm down," he playfully stated. "I need to see what the pussy tastes like."

"It takes good," she said, and looked over her shoulder at him. "Exactly like you told me you liked it."

Bringing his hand up near his mouth, he sniffed the one that he had let trail across her anus and didn't smell a pronounced smell of doo-doo, nor did he smell anything fowl coming from the one he'd just had inside of her.

Putting the one he had inside of her in his mouth, he tasted a hint of lime and took it out.

"You like?" she asked, as she straightened back up.

"I love it," he replied, and added "lean back over. I wanna eat it from the back. I'm a introduce you to some shit you ain't never had done to you."

"Like what?" she asked, as she leaned back over.

"I'm a eat that ass," he replied, and lowered down to a squatting position so that his face was level with her ass.

Show me," she purred, and closed her eyes in anticipation of the ride that was to come. A ride she hoped she would remember long after it was done.

CHAPTER 3

Running the lighter from one end of the blunt to the other. Fish stood on the spring-board of the set of logs behind Lippert Street with a half-grin as Phil, Hub, Shed and Cee all laughed at his story about how he had freckled-faced, blond-haired, Rebecca in the back hallway of her building last night, with her dress up around her waist and her cotton panties tossed off to the side. What had them dying laughing was him telling them how he was five-minutes into eating her from the back when a horrific odor came out of her that almost made him throw up inside of her.

"You nasty as shit," Cee said, his black curls bouncing on his slim-shoulders as he shook with laughter.

"Yo, I'd a body-shot that hoe," Hub stated.

Putting the blunt in the side of his mouth, Fish said "and when Unc came for you then what?" Unc was Rebecca's twenty-three year old man, who was five-nine and strong as a bull. And on top of that, he was a golden-glove boxer as well. At five-eleven, a hundred and forty-pounds, slinging hands wasn't Fish's style. Even though he didn't style himself as a hustler he kept his trademark .380 close at hand when he was out here on these streets. He lived in the roughest projects in the entire state, so he knew that he had to be ready for whatever.

"Getting' knocked the fuck out, that's what," Phil said by way of a reply for Hub, and they all knew that was true.

Though Cee was the oldest at seventeen, Hub was the biggest, even though Shed had the most heart. At five-eight and an even two-hundred pounds, he was indeed a big boy. But there was a difference between big and mostly fat, which Hub was, and big and mostly muscle, which Unc was.

"You'd of been down for the twenty-count," Shed said, now laughing at what Phil had just said. To Fish he said "bet you won't go back and get no more of that though."

Taking his time to make sure that the blunt lit evenly Fish took a few pulls on it before taking it out of his mouth to look at it. "Shit, I ain't even get none then," he said, once he saw that the blunt was evenly lit. "By the time I got done retchin' I was done. Shit, she was so embarrassed that she kept tryin to blow me to make up for it."

"I'd of definitely let her big titty ass do that," Shed said.

"That's cause you had it before," Fish said, stepping off of the spring-board and handing Shed the blunt. "Shit, while you frontin' you're the reason I even went after her in the first place."

Grabbing the blunt, Shed said "it wasn't like that when I hit it," and then took a hard pull and passed it to Phil who was sitting right next to him.

"I heard it was right," Phil said, while getting the blunt situated in his fingers.

"My brother hit," Cee said, while watching Phil to make sure that he didn't take any more than two hits.

"That black muthafucka ain't fuck no Rebecca," Hub said, not even trying to hear that. Goop, Cee's brother, was black and ugly as a muthafucka. And even though he was a few years older than them, they all knew that he messed with nothing but ugly women.

"Did too," Cee said, and then added "he hit last summer."

"Man, ain't no bad ass Rebecca give his ugly ass no pussy," Fish said, agreeing with Hub. He had put in a lot of work on the side to make that happen, and in his mind her giving Goop some cheapened his accomplishment. At sixteen, he had bagged a bad nineteen-year old white-chick who had a man. Though she wasn't his first older chick, she was of the few that was of bragging material.

"Whatever," Cee said, not wanting to keep up the dumb argument, even though he knew that it was true. Goop had left the door cracked so he could watch, but he didn't wanna say anything because he knew they would clown him for being a freak even though every last one of them would have watched too. "Nigga pass the blunt," he said to Phil, who was trying to hit it again for the third time.

"Hawkin' ass Nigga," Phil said, and took a quick hit before passing Cee the blunt.

Wanting to say something to Cee's dismissive "whatever," Fish instead let it go. He could care less about the funky pussy hoe. What had him mad was Cee pressing the issue when everybody knew that none of the bad shorties in the hood even gave his brother the time of day. Cool, he said to himself, and started plotting on how he was going to get Cee back for trying to steal his shine. He did have a badass girlfriend whose skin-tone matched her name. Penny. And Penny's badass had a good friend that he was already crushing on the low. A good friend who would do just about anything for him.

CHAPTER 4

Leaving the smoke-session with Shed, mainly because he didn't want to go down to the bottom of the hill where all of the hustlers were hanging out at, Fish said "what's up, you trynah shoot down to Mail Court and see what's up with Veronica and 'em?"

"Why we headed up the hill then?" Shed asked, as they crossed Lippert Street on their way up to Hutchinson, which was in the opposite direction from Mail Court.

Looking at his gold-plated Timex watch and seeing that it was ten-after six, Fish said "something I'm tryin to see up this way."

"What?" Shed asked, though what he really should have said was "who," because whatever Fish was on he knew had something to do with a girl.

I'm checkin' to see if my bun-buns is out by the hoop court," Fish replied, lying. He was looking dead at Penny and Colleen's row-house building, and neither one of them were in site of their apartment, or the front area where they usually hung out at so he was hoping that they were around the hoop-court or the hill over-looking it, which was just now coming into view.

Ready to say that he didn't hear anybody up on the court, which was about forty-feet up ahead and to their left, Shed decided not to say anything. There were only five girls on this end of Hutchinson and Griffin that could be Fish's bun-buns. Penny, who was Cee's woman, and definitely not his bun-buns because she was way to square to cheat on him. Big titty, no ass, Colleen, who was a jump-off for the older crowd since she was nineteen. Her sister Callie, who was a year younger than them and learning well from her sister. Trina, who word had it was hitting the glass dick and had started trading pussy for rocks, and badass red-bone Tameka, whose apartment they were just now passing.

As they came up the hill Fish looked towards the basketball court and parking lot behind it and saw that it was empty of even the kids that were usually out playing up this way. Looking up to the swing-set he saw that it too was empty, that and wondered what was going on? It was like sixty-five degrees out and one of those days in April where it wasn't raining, and virtually nobody was out playing or kicking it.

"Ain't nobody up here," Shed said, as they continued on.

"Let's shoot up Callie's," Fish said.

"You on yah own. Don't be tryin to pawn me off on no Colleen," Shed said, knowing that Fish had been hitting Callie on the low, but not Colleen.

"You know she can suck a dick through a pixie-straw, right?" Fish asked.

"I heard," Shed replied, while nodding his head. "But I'm cool. She's a little too heavy for me," he added, not liking his women heavy-set, which Colleen was. But her DD's, along with her cute-face, did have him thinking about it.

"Cool," Fish said, and they walked across the lawn up to the sidewalk. Following Fish up the few steps that lead to her door, Shed said "don't even try it," as Fish knocked on the door.

As many times as you set me up, cut it out," Fish said, grinning as he added "Dog-Town," with no need to say anything else further. Shed had bagged a bad mixed girl name Miranda, who had the only red-bone ugly friend Fish had ever seen. So that Shed could hit Miranda Fish had to hit the ugly girl.

"Who is it?" they both heard Coleen say.

"Fish," he replied.

Opening the door Colleen said "Callie's not here," before she saw Shed and said "hey Shed."

"What's up," Shed said, his tone detached so as not to make it sound like a question.

"Where yah peoples at?" Fish asked, while looking into the living room and not seeing anyone.

"Gone," Colleen replied.

"Cool, cause I need to holla at you," Fish said, and then turned to give Shed some dap and said "in a minute."

"In a minute," Shed said, shaking his hand and then leaving without saying anything to her.

Letting Fish come in, Colleen shut the door and said "why is he so rude?"

"Shit, you know why," Fish replied, grinning as he went to sit down.

"Don't start," she said, while rolling her eyes. Going to sit down across from him, she said "what is it?"

"Penny," Fish replied, and let his eyes lower to her breasts.

"Cee's Penny?" she dubiously asked.

"Yeah."

"And what do you want with her?" she asked, sure that he wasn't about to ask her to hook him up with her. But then again this was Fish so who knew what he might want.

"I need you to help me get cool with her," he replied, his grin turning into a smile because he knew what she was thinking.

Smiling, mainly because she thought he was playing, she said "boy, you know she's not giving you the time of day."

"I'm not tryin to hit. I just wanna get cool with her," he said.

"Then come up when Cee comes up," she said, the look on her face saying what she wasn't vocalizing. That she didn't believe a word that he had just said.

"I am, but I wanna hang out when yah'll be hanging out to," he said, and by the look on her face he knew that he had just threw her on that reply. He definitely couldn't be trying to hit if he was coming up with her man to hang out.

"I don't believe you," she finally said, mainly because she was at a loss for anything else to say. The Fish that she knew was all about having sex. He was the only person that she had slept with that had also slept with her sister, but after listening to her muffled moans for well over thirty-minutes her soaked panties and engorged clitoris had sealed the deal.

Busting out laughing, he said, "straight talk. Trust me. Just help me get to know her."

"Alright Fish," she finally said, though she knew that it had to be more to it then what he was letting on.

16

CHAPTER 5

Leaving Colleen's, Fish headed to the circle, while noting that the sun was setting which meant that he had about thirty-minutes before he needed to start heading home for dinner, but he wanted to run down to the circle and see if Shed was at his spot first. Taking the back-stairway behind the building he came out from in between them and on to Lippert where he saw Brutus and Danny Boy standing on the corner of Lippert to his left and his cousin Chops, Dirty D, Goop, and T-Love leaning against the wooden rail in front of Shed's three-story apartment building kicking it to his right.

Not making it five-steps towards Chops, Fish heard Brutus say "There's that bitch-ass nigga right there," the tone of his voice causing him to stop and turn and see who he was talking about because that tone said that Brutus was about to give somebody the business. The Brutus pound-out, stomp-out business.

"Yeah, I'm talkin' to yo bitch-ass nigga," Brutus said, and pointed at Fish to make sure that he knew exactly who he was talking about, as his six-four strides started eating up the twenty yards separating them.

Not knowing what his problem was, though he figured it had something to do with Dionne, who was Brutus's baby momma that Fish had been creeping with for well over a year, Fish took a step back and his hand shot under his Pelle' Pelle shirt and pulled his baby-boy out. Pointing it at Brutus, who stopped dead in his tracks upon seen the gun, he said "you call me one moe bitch and I'm a push yo shit back."

"Woe, easy with that now," Danny Boy said, having been trailing Brutus until he saw Fish pull the gun out and was now moving out of the line of fire.

Moving the gun over to Danny Boy and then back to Brutus, Fish said "fall back."

"Hey, hey, I'm cool," Danny Boy said, while taking a step back with his hands raised up. "Let's ride Brute," he said, ready to go. They didn't have a gun between them so as far as he was concerned this fight was over. Especially since Chops and their crew were on their way down the street. And he knew they kept guns on them.

"Nah, ain't no goin' nowhere," Fish said, locking eyes with Brutus.

"What's up fam," Chops said, as he came up beside Fish.

"Trynah figure out what this dummy's trippin on before I light his ass up," Fish replied.

"Nigga, you fucked my bitch," Brutus said, staring daggers at Fish. If it wasn't for the gun he would be tearing into his ass right now, and Chops and them be damned.

"Dionne?" Fish asked, his face twisted up in disbelief.

"Yeah nigga, and don't act like you didn't either. She already told me," Brutus spat, his fists now balled up.

Turning the gun so that it was pointed at him sideways, Fish said "I ain't fuck yo bitch, she fucked me."

18

"Oh shit!" Dirty D exclaimed, and busted out laughing, followed by T-Love.

"She took the head and the dick when I tole'er I was cool," Fish said, and was ready to tell him she had been taking it the whole time they were together, but changed his mind. "So why you trippin on me, fuck nigga, you need to be trippin on that hoe."

"Aye yo, yah'll need to chill," Goop said. He knew Brutus, and knew that he was one or two smart comments away from charging Fish, who would more than likely bust him. But, by the way, Brutus was looking, it wouldn't surprise him if the bullets didn't do anything to him.

"Yeah, ya'll need to chill," Danny Boy said, while moving over until he was beside Brutus, the whole time keeping his hands in the air. "Let's go dog," he said, and moved in front of him and locked eyes with him. He knew that he wanted to get at Fish despite the gun. If the shoe was on the other foot, he would have to. That smart-ass comment about Brutus's girl taking the dick would've ended up with Fish either busting him or him taking the gun from him and beating the shit out of him with it.

Looking around Danny Boy, Brutus said "fuck you and that hoe. Bitch! That's why I punished that bitch!"

Laughing, Fish said "nah, fuck yo tender-dick ass. You 'bout to die over a hoe fuckin' half the hood."

"Let's go dog," Danny Boy said, now spreading his arms wide and crowding Brutus to make him back up. "Chill bra," he added, and forcefully bumped him with his chest.

Letting Danny boy back Brutus up, Fish lowered the gun and looked at him with a smirk, as if he was saying now what?

"Chill, let's go," Chops said, as he put his hand on Fish's shoulder. "Let that go."

"I'm cool," Fish said, though not taking his eyes off Brutus, who was still being backed up by Danny Boy.

"You know you better watch your back," Dirty D said.

"True, true," T-Love stated.

"Fuck that nigga," Fish said, as Brutus finally turned around at the corner and headed towards the bottom of the hill with Danny Boy. "Nigga trippin over a hoe everybody fucking," he added.

"Shit, I ain't fuckin her," Dirty D said, and looked to T-Love. "You hittin' dog?"

"Nah," T-Love replied, while slightly shaking his head.

"Me neither," Goop said, smiling.

"Ya'll know what I mean," Fish said, grinning.

"Dog, you can't fuck every hoe in the hood," Chops said, as they all turned to walk back to where they were chilling at.

Smiling, Fish said "says who?" and they all shared a laugh that eased the tension of the last few minutes. As far as he was concerned, the only reason he was getting so much pussy was because niggas wasn't handling their business. Wasn't his fault that hoes mouths ran like water, and his name was always in their mouths.

CHAPTER 6

After smoking a few blunts with everybody, Shed walked with Fish towards Fish's crib so he could eat dinner with his mother before she went to work. "You, you know we gotta get at 'em right?" Shed asked, as they crossed Griffin Street. He didn't know why Fish was acting like everything was cool. From what he had heard how Fish had stunted on Brutus he had to know that Brutus was coming back. No way was he taking that lying down and living over here with no reputation.

"Fuck that nigga," Fish said, though his eyes were constantly moving from the row-houses on their left to the three-story apartment buildings on the right, as well as the cut coming up at the end of both buildings to make sure that nobody was laying on him. "That nigga knows I'm a pop his top if he comes back on that stupid shit."

"Nigga, you trippin," Shed stated. "Cut the jokes. You know he's comin' back strapped," he said, even though he had never heard about Brutus getting mixed up in gunplay. But for Brutus to come back without a strap would be suicide.

"I ain't stuntin 'em," Fish said, not letting Shed get him geesed up to go and chase down a murder-case. Niggas in jail were getting absolutely no pussy, and if everything went bad that's exactly, where he would end up. And if it didn't then his and Brutus' people would be beefing, and that definitely wouldn't end well. Shit, if Brutus would've pushed the issue in the circle Chops would've gunned him down to. And if Danny Boy didn't like it then he'd of caught an overdose of lead as well.

"Man," Shed said in frustration.

"It's cool," Fish stated, trying to get Shed to calm down. "I'm in for the night anyway, so it's cool man."

"You trippin," Shed stated, his over-sized bottom lip trembling in frustration. True, it was Fish's situation, but he was ready to ride. But if Fish was cool with being snuck then he had to be cool with it he said to himself, and they made the rest of the walk to Fish's crib in silence.

Stopping in front of his crib, Fish gave Shed some dap and said, "I'm a see you in the morning."

Dapping him back up, Shed said "I'm a be at the bottom of the hill. If I hear somethin' I'll call and let you know what's up."

"In a minute," Fish said, and headed in the house.

Looking out of the kitchen as Fish came through the front door, his mother said "what did I tell you about having them lil' girls calling here like they pay my phone bill?"

"I didn't," Fish replied, as he shut the door while wondering who was calling.

"That little ignorant ass Dionne has been calling here every twenty or thirty minutes like she done lost her damn mind," she said, while turning to get his plate. "I know I'm about to call Quita and tell her to get her daughter in check if she keeps this dumb-shit up."

"Wasn't me," Fish stated, and turned towards the steps to go upstairs and call her to see what type of time she was on.

"What in the hell is she doing calling you like that?" she asked.

"I don't know, but she's tryna get some dumb shit started between me and Brutus so I'm 'bout to check her and see what she's trippin on," he replied, and started up the steps until she motioned for him to stop.

"Big Danny's boy?" she asked, and grew nervous when he nodded his head in reply.

"I got this though. It ain't nutin'. Go 'head and get our plates together. By the time you're done I'll be down," he said, and hurried up the steps. Going to his room, he sat on the bed and picked his phone book up from beside the phone and went to Dionne's number, and then picked them up phone and dialed it.

"Hello," he heard Dionne nervously say.

"What kinda game you playin?" he asked with attitude in his tone.

"I'm sorry Fish. You don't understand," she replied, fighting not to break down and start crying again.

"You muthafuckin' right I don't understand why you got me out here ready to lay that nigga out over some shit you put me in the middle of," he said, not trying to hear that. "How you gone even come out yah mouth and tell that nigga we crushin' anyway?" he asked, not understanding how his name even came out of her mouth in the first place.

"Remember last year when me and him broke up because I caught him cheating on me with Tina?" she asked, and then continued on without waiting for an answer because she knew that he did because they had spent some of that time together. "He wasn't helping me take care of Carlton, so I went to Child Support on him," she said, and paused to gather her strength to continue. "He made them do a blood test and the tests came back this morning."

When she stopped all of a sudden, he wanted to say "and," but some inner-instinct told him to hold his tongue. Or maybe it was good common sense that put two and two together. Brutus was tripping over way more than him hitting Dionne. He was tripping over the fact that his son wasn't his son, and Dionne had said some dumb shit.

"Carlton's not his son," she finally said, and started crying. "He's yours."

"Woe, woe, woe," Fish said, now shocked. "I know you ain't tell that nigga no fuck-shit like that?"

"He made me," she replied between sobs. "He wouldn't stop hittin me. And he tore up everything here. I'm about to go over my mothers and stay. The only reason I'm still here is because I was waiting on you to call."

"You tryna make me kill 'em," he sadly stated, and did the only thing he could under the circumstance. He hung up. He knew this wasn't going to have a happy ending regardless of whether or not he was the kids father. Brutus thought he was, and there was only one way this was going to end. Somebody was going to get hurt really, really bad.

For a long five-minutes, he just sat there with his head in his hand really thinking about nothing. This was bad, and he knew he needed to get away from it, but couldn't figure out how. Finally, he rose and took his .380 from his belt and went to the closet and took the shoebox down that he kept his guns in. Taking the lid off of it he set it on top of his thirteen-inch black and white television and looked inside of the box at his midnight black .45 caliber Smith & Weston.

Looking at it a feeling of sadness washed over him. He had said that he would never carry it unless it was going down, and he knew that time was drawing near. Putting the .380 beside of it, he picked the lid up and put it back on top of the box and put it back on the shelf. Standing there looking at the box for a few-seconds he finally turned and headed down stairs to eat dinner with his mother.

CHAPTER 7

When none of his peoples didn't show-up, or call, by ten o'clock Fish figured that none of them knew what was really going on so he went upstairs and took the .45 out of the shoe-box, along with a spare-clip. Putting on his Chicago Bulls hoodie, he put the .45 inside of the hoodie pocket. Putting the extra-clip in his pants pocket he was ready to put the shoebox back on the shelf when he decided that he might as well take the .380 too, and put it back in his waistband where he normally carried it.

Looking out of the front window to make sure that everything was clear, he saw Fats and his older sister Slick sitting in front of their building and left the house. Him and Fats were cool, and he knew that he wouldn't just stand-by and let Brutus dog him. And like Shed, he was a little goon in the making. Even the older dudes respected his gangster.

"What's up," Fish said, as he made his way across the street towards the stairs that was in between Fat's building and the one to his left that would take him down to the back of Mail Court.

"Hey lover boy," Slick playfully stated.

"What's up my nigga," Fast said, waving Fish over. "Let me holla at you for a minute."

"Aight," Fish said, but stopped to look all of the way around to make sure that Brutus wasn't laying in wait on him. Going over to where they sat, he said "what's up," by way of greeting, though he blessed Slick with his trademark grin that showed off his dimples. Her high-yellow ass was fine as hell.

"Quit smiling at my sistah like 'at nigga," Fats jokingly said, while standing to give Fish some dap.

"He can smile at me anytime he wants too," Slick playfully said, and batted her eyelashes at him and smiled right back at him as she stood and tossed the butt of her Newport to the side.

Dapping Fats up, Fish said "she's cool," while locking eyes with her to see if she was serious or just playing.

"You've got enough female problems nigga," Fats said, releasing Fish's hand.

"And I can't wait to learn all of the sordid details," Slick said, while turning to go back inside of the hallway.

"Bye," Fats said, waving her on.

Laughing, Fish said "so what's the word?"

"He's sayin' he gone fuck you around," Fats replied, and then went on to tell him about the argument that Brutus and Chops had gotten into at the bottom of the hill that ended with Brutus flashing Chops a strap to let him know that he ready for whatever.

Nodding his head, mainly at the statement about Brutus being strapped, Fish said "you know where Shed's at?"

"Last time I saw 'em he was under the shelter with Kunta and Hub," Fish replied. "I'm sayin though, what you gone do?"

"I'm definitely not gone run," Fish replied.

"You just might wanna be easy and let shit blow over though," Fats said. "That nigga can't be mad forever dog."

If you knew what I knew you'd re-think that, Fish said to himself, a bit surprised that Slick didn't already know what was really going on since her and Dionne ran in the same circles. "I ain't looking for 'em, but I ain't duckin' either," he said.

"I feel you my nigga," Fats said, and extended his hand to Fish and they dapped up and he pulled him in for a manly hug. It was then that he felt the gun in Fish's hoodie-pocket, as well as the strap on his waist. Patting him on the back, he said "don't get trapped off on no shit you can get around," he said, and released him.

"I'm not," Fish said, and released him as well.

"In a minute."

"In a minute," Fats said, and watched Fish turn and head to the end of the building.

Stopping about five-feet from the edge of the building, gripping the pistol in his hoodie-pocket with his finger on the trigger, Fish quickly took three-steps to the edge of the building prepared to bust Brutus or anybody else laying on him, but saw no one. Exhaling in relief, he cut across the grass towards the dirt path leading down the little hill to the back of Mail Court.

Stopping at the top of the path, he looked at the back of Fat's building to make sure that nobody was hiding back there, and then towards the back of the building to his left and saw that it was clear. Looking to the building in front of him, he looked down it, wishing that he could see inside of the back hallways to make sure that nobody was hiding back there as well. It was three-stories of hallways in each apartment building so anybody could be hiding in the hallways.

Not seeing anything out of the ordinary, he continued on down the path that went down at a ninety-degree incline for about ten-yards that ended at a drainage ditch that had a sidewalk on the other side that wrapped around the side of the building. Reaching the bottom of the path, he jumped across the ditch. As he reached the zenith of his jump he heard a grunt, followed by the pitter-patter of running foot-steps, and quickly looked to his left where the sounds where coming from and saw Brutus and Danny Boy coming out of the back-hallway at a dead-run trying to eat up the fifteen-yards that separated them from Fish as quickly as possible.

With one hand out to balance himself because the other was still in his pocket holding the gun, Fish knew that he was in trouble. The barrel of the gun was pointed in the opposite direction. He also knew that if he didn't do something quick he was about to receive the pounding of his life because he wouldn't be able to out-run them like this. So, with no other choice, he did the only thing he could under the circumstances. No sooner than his front-foot touched the ground he pulled the trigger twice, and two loud booms came from inside of his hoodie in rapid succession.

Knowing that they had the drop on Fish, Brutus had left is gun at the small of his back. He really didn't want to kill him, he just wanted to beat his balls to a pulp. Literally. But the sound of the gunfire caused him to flinch and duck, imagining bullets coming at him. All of which slowed his and Danny Boy's forward momentum roughly five-yards from Fish.

No sooner than his second-foot hit the ground Fish pulled the trigger, a third time and then poured on as much speed as he could. He didn't know if the shots would be enough to get him away, but he was giving it all he had.

Not hearing any bullets wheezing by their heads from the first shots, Danny Boy ignored the third-shot and ran around Brutus, who had all but stopped. As far as he was concerned, they were getting this nigga now.

Putting on every ounce of speed that he could muster with his hand still inside of his hoodie, Fish took off down the side of the building. Looking over his shoulder he saw Danny Boy hurrying around Brutus and tried to pump his legs faster, but his awkward gate was holding him back.

"Bring yo ass here," Danny Boy said, as he closed on Fish, who was now about six-yards in front of him. Unlike Brutus, he still had his gun in his hand, and at the first sign of Fish even attempting to turn and point his at him he was opening fire

Seeing that he wasn't going to be able to out-run Danny Boy as long as he kept his hand inside of his pocket, and not wanting to release his hold on the gun incase Danny Boy did chase him down, Fish threw caution to the wind. As he turned the corner of the building, and was momentarily out of site, Danny Boy, he pulled the gun while praying that it didn't get stuck on the pocket.

Turning the corner not five-steps behind Fish, ready to power back up to full speed and close the deal, Danny Boy saw Fish's head whip around. So intent was he on catching him that he didn't see the arm whip around right behind it until the last second. It was then that he thought about shooting Fish, but his stride was all wrong. The gun was up by his head, with the barrel pointing up and away.

So when he saw flame leap from the barrel of Fish's gun he did the only thing he could, he turned to the right in hopes of getting on Fish's far side away from the gun. As the first-boom reached its apex, and started to die down, Danny Boy felt his left leg punched out from under him as a second-boom reached his ears. Because he'd just put his weight on it the force of the slug drove his left-leg into his right and caused him to go down.

"Oh!" Danny Boy exclaimed, right before the side of his head hit the cement and the gun went flying as his vision filled with stars.

Seeing Danny Boy go down, Fish looked back to the corner of the building and saw Brutus coming around it. Not even giving him time to think about what he wanted to do he sent two-slugs at him, both having the desired effect. He hurried right back around the corner.

CHAPTER 8

Coming off of Mail Court on to Copenhagen Drive at a dead-run, Fish didn't slow down until he saw a bunch of people standing in the middle of the street up by the shelter and knew who at least one of them was. Chops. He didn't see Shed in the crowd, but that was alright. Chops was there. Glancing behind him to make sure that neither Brutus nor Danny Boy was following him, it was then that he noticed that his .380 wasn't on his waistband. Fuck, he mentally said to himself, as he put his .45 back in his hoodie-pocket.

"What happened?" Chops asked, stepping out of the crowd.

"Brutus and Danny Boy tried to jump me," Fish replied, out of breath. "I lit Danny Boy's ass up though. Where's Shed at ?" he asked, not seeing him.

"Up Turtle's," Dirty D replied.

"Snatch 'em up for me," Chops said to Dirty D. Looking back to Fish, he said "where you hit Danny Boy at?"

"I don't know," Fish replied, and bent over and put his hands on his knees to catch his breath.

"What about Brutus?" T-Love asked.

"Coward ass nigga got somewhere when I started bustin' at 'em," Fish replied, and then told them how they had tried to sneak him while he was coming down the path.

"Shit, they couldn't of gotten far. Let's finish this shit tonight," Chops said.

I need to catch my breath, Fish wanted to say, but knew that he couldn't. If he showed any hesitation now he would be in trouble. Instead, he said "let's ride."

Ready to holler and stop Dirty D, Chops stopped what he was about to say as they all heard multiple sirens. Turning, along with everybody else, to face the front of the

Woo, he had a feeling that those sirens were on their way there.

"They're coming," Fish nervously said. "Let's ride cuz."

Seeing the police-cars come into view through the trees that obscured their vision somewhat, Chops said "lets shoot up Turtles," and they all quick-walked on to Bowman Court as the police cars raced through the intersection and headed across the bridge. Heading down the Court now at a faster walk he saw Dirty D go in Turtles building and he quickened the pace.

Going into the apartment, Chops said "I need the back-bedroom."

"Well hello to you to," Turtle sarcastically stated, as everybody trooped in behind him. Seeing Fish her sarcastic look changed to a bright smile and she said "hey lover boy."

"What's up?" Shed said, coming into the living room.

"Damn, does everybody know what's going on?" Fish asked, while sadly shaking his head.

"Probably not that you're a father, but by tomorrow they will," she replied, and saw everybody turn to look at Fish with their jaws on the floor. "What?" she innocently asked. "I guess yah'll didn't know, huh?"

"You got Dionne pregnant?" Shed asked, shocked.

"I didn't hear that," Turtle replied.

"He wasn't talkin to you Turtle," Fish quickly said in hopes of cutting her off before she spilled more of the beans.

"Oh shit," Chops said, quickly putting two and two together. If Dionne wasn't pregnant and only had one kid then that meant that, the kid was Fish's and not Brutus's.

"Know what?" Dirty D asked, still not getting it.

"Dionne's son is his not Brutus's," Turtle said by way of a reply that earned a withering-glare from Fish.

"That nigga's gone kill you," T-Love stated.

"Damn," both Dirty D and Goop said at the same time.

"Come on," Chops said, and led the way to the back bedroom that Turtle rented out for the hustlers to handle business in.

No sooner than the door was shut, Fish said "cuz, I just found out when I was at the crib."

"When was you gone tell us?" Chops asked, still trying to wrap his mind around it.

"You was hittin that long?" Goop asked, impressed.

"Since I was fourteen," Fish replied, while nodding his head, figuring that Goop's question was the better one to answer because had Turtle not said anything then he wouldn't have either.

"That nigga gone kill you," Dirty D said, sure that Brutus was either going to kill Fish or Fish was going to kill Brutus.

"We gotta get 'em," Shed said.

"Nah," T-Love said, and paused to shake his head. "You gotta get 'em," he said, looking at Fish. Looking to Chops, he said "he wasn't going to tell you. We can't ride on this one."

Looking from T-Love to Fish, Chops wanted to say something, but couldn't find the right thing to say. He knew he couldn't leave Fish on his own. Even with Shed, the two of them might not be enough to handle Brutus. And he knew that if Brutus kept pushing the issue, he would come back with his brother, H-Bomb, and when H-Bomb came, Fort was coming right behind him.

"Fuck!" Chops finally said, and needed to lash out at something so he hit the wall with the side of his fist.

"I can handle it cuz," Fish said. "I got it."

"You ain't no killah," Chops said, mean mugging him. Looking to T-Love, he said "he's my blood."

"Who wasn't going to tell you," T-Love said, while nodding his head. A nod that said that he could ride, but the Four Horseman wouldn't be riding along with him.

CHAPTER 9

At a couple of minutes till eleven Fish and Shed left Turtles crib knowing more than they did when they had come. Danny Boy had been shot in the leg, and was in stable condition at the hospital. Brutus had went with him, but was now back in the Woo. Turtle couldn't find out where, but she did tell Fish that Dionne wasn't at her apartment. Once word spread about the shooting, she had left. As far as Turtle could find out Dionne wasn't even in the projects.

"Where do you think he's at?" Fish asked, as they walked down the last flight of stairs, both now with their hands on their guns.

"We gone find out," Shed replied, and paused at the bottom of the steps to make sure that he was hearing what he thought he was hearing. Nothing. He wasn't hearing any voices, and at a little after eleven that wasn't right. Bowman Court was on Copenhagen Drive, which was the main hustling spot in the Woo. At eleven o'clock on Saturday night, it should have been noisy. Taking his gun out, he motioned Fish to hold on and went to the closed hallway door and looked out of the eight-inch wide windowless window in the door.

"What's up?" Fish asked in a low-voice, his gun also now in his hand.

"I don't see nuthin'," Shed replied, and placed his hand on the bar and slowly pushed it in so that he could open the

36

door quietly. He didn't know what was going on out there, but he wanted to move silently until he found out.

Slowly pushing the door open, he looked through the crack to make sure that no one was laying on them from back of the Court before pushing it open some more so he could see more of the front of the Court. Stopping it when he had it open about a foot, he switched to the window and what he saw in the parking lot across the street froze him. It also explained why no one was out. Parked in the parking lot, side-by-side, were two police cars.

"The cops. They're in the parking-lot," Shed said, and slowly let the door close. "We gotta go out the back way."

"Aight," Fish said, and they retraced their steps back up to Turtles apartment and told everybody about the police outside.

"They probably got the whole hood on smash," Good said.

"How we find out?" Shed asked.

"When you go out of the back shoot up the steps and look out of the cut up to the circle. If they're lockin' the hood down they gone have cars somewhere up that way," Goop replied.

"They gone have 'em all over if they're doin that," Chops stated.

"Which means ain't gone be nothin goin on," Turtle said. "So all of yah'll can take your young asses home and let everything cool down."

"She's right," Chops stated, mainly because he didn't want Fish and Shed out looking for Brutus without him. "If they all over the hood ain't nuthin' jumpin' off."

Looking to Fish, Shed said "let's make sure they out like that first."

"Aight," Fish replied.

CHAPTER 10

After leaving Turtle's, Fish and Shed had soon found out that there were police all over the Woo, so they called it a night and both headed home. Before going in Fish snuck back down to Mail Court to see if he could find his gun, but couldn't find it. He didn't know if he had dropped it while running down Griffin, but couldn't go and see because the police were still parked out in the parking lot.

Laying down with his gun right beside of him0 under the covers, it felt like no, sooner than he'd closed his eyes and drifted off to sleep than he was being smacked awake.

"Get your dumb-ass up," Ms. Pat angrily stated, smacked him again across the cheek.

Shocked awake, Fish went for his gun in hopes of getting Brutus off of him. He didn't know how he'd gotten into his apartment, but he knew that if he didn't do something fast he was as good as dead.

"You want this?" she asked, and smacked him upside of the head with one hand while raising his gun with the other one.

"Mom?" he asked, while covering his head in hopes of warding off anymore blows, while praying that that was her voice he'd just heard.

"Luckily for your stupid ass it is," she replied, and stepped back and turned the light on. "Get your ass dressed and downstairs before I light into your ass for real," she said, and tossed him his gun back. "And that better not be the gun you shot him with either," she menacingly stated, before turning and leaving. Shaking his head and exhaling, Fish again shook his head and then got out of bed. He hadn't been expecting her home until early in the morning. Obviously, somebody had called and told her what had happened because she'd left work early to come home. Getting up, he went to use the bathroom and wash his face before going downstairs.

No sooner than Fish came down the steps, she said "start at the beginning and don't leave anything out," as she sat on the sofa. A wave of anger rolling off of her so clear that he had to see it.

"Brutus and Danny boy tried to jump me and I shot Danny Boy in the leg so I could get away," he replied.

"Now you must think I'm ten-karat stupid," she said, the look on her face telling him to quit playing with her. "I said start from the beginning. They just didn't try and jump you for no reason. And don't act like I don't know he's Dionne's boyfriend either," she said, and pointed a finger at him. "Let me find out you're the new neighborhood Jody?" she asked, her eyes now lowered to slits.

"Momma, Dionne did some dumb shit," Fish said, and stopped to gather his courage to tell her about the baby.

"Boy, both of you all did some dumb shit. You've been sleeping together and now he's found out," she said, and motioned him to go on.

"It's worse than that," he said, and plopped down on the sofa.

"Plop on my muthafuckin sofa one more time and it is going to be way worse than that," she said, wanting to get up and smack the taste out of his mouth she was so mad.

"They just found out that Brutus isn't the dad of her baby. She told 'em I was," he finally said.

"Oh sweet Jesus," she stated, her head falling back to the back of the couch. "Is it true?"

"She said they did some tests and it said that he wasn't the father," Fish replied, while shrugging a shoulder. "I don't know if it's mines, but she said it wasn't his."

"Boy," she said, the word being exhaled out in a long breath. "I told you about that thing between your legs, but you wouldn't listen. You just wouldn't listen," she sadly stated, the last part coming out in a pain-filled sigh.

CHAPTER 11

Sleeping until a little after nine Fish awoke with a sense of fore boding. A feeling so strong that the harder he tried to shake it the more it gripped his heart. At one point he tried to roll back over and go to sleep, but knew it was a lost cause. The feeling was just too deep in him. Taking a deep breath, he rolled over and picked the phone up and dialed Shed's number.

"Hello," he heard Shed's mother say.

"Good morning Ms. C. Is Shed home?" he asked.

"Hold on," she replied, and hollered for Shed to pick up the phone.

Coming on the line, Shed said "I got it mah," and they both heard her click off.

"She that mad at me?" Fish asked.

"Both of us," Shed replied. "Should've seen how she cussed me out when this morning."

"I guess I won't be coming to your spot for the day," Fish jokingly stated, and then told him about last night with his mother.

"I'm definitely not coming over yours," Shed said, and they both busted out laughing. After the laughter was done, he said "what's the move though? We finishin' this or what?"

"Give me an hour and meet me up on Hutchinson behind my spot," Fish replied.

"I'm there," Shed stated.

CHAPTER 12

It took an Act of Congress to get his mother to let him leave the house, but when he did Fish went out of the back door and went up the stairs to Hutchinson Street where he saw Shed leaning on the fence waiting on him.

"What it do?" Shed asked, pushing off of the fence and coming towards Fish.

"Tell me you got some blunts?" Fish asked, and they shook hands.

"Nah, but let's hit the store," Shed replied. "I need to get right anyway after the shit momma put me through."

"Shit, don't feel alone," Fish said, and turned around and they retraced his steps down the stairs and went between the buildings out on to Lippert Street. "You know I hit that too, right?" he said, as they headed towards the path that he had taken down the little hill last night where Brutus and Danny Boy had tried to sneak him.

"Who?" Shed asked.

"Ebony," Fish replied, and grinned.

"Say word?" Shed asked, not thinking that Fish was going to get her, even though she had been flirting with him.

"Word," Fish replied. "And I'm tellin' you, you got to get some of that. She's a stone-cold freak."

"Say word?" Shed asked, now smiling from ear to ear. Nobody had really heard much of anything about Ebony's sex-game so what he was saying was music to his ears.

"Bra, listen to me. We didn't even make it out of the kitchen. I ate that shit with her leaned over the kitchen-chair, and she sucked my shit with some whip-cream on it."

"Oh," Shed exclaimed, and started running in place. "I got to get me some of that."

"It was like that," Fish said, laughing at Shed's antics. "I'm supposed to slide back through and see what's up tomorrow."

"Shit, take her to the crib so I can hide in the closet," Shed said, and Fish busted out laughing.

"You nasty muthafucka," Fish said, laughing even harder. True, they had done that before, but that was like two-years ago when they were coming into their own. Now, they were older and the thought of his man watching him do it wasn't all that cool.

"Shit, call it what you want, but I'm trynah see her bad ass naked," Shed said, as they started down the path.

"Let me see what I can do," Fish said, his gaze turning to his right as Shed looked to his left. This was where they'd caught him slipping last night and he wasn't about to let that happen again. This time he had the barrel of his gun pointed in the right direction so if anybody came out of the hallway this time he wouldn't just be firing for effects. He would be shooting to kill. That's exactly what his father had told him to do this morning when he called to see what had happened.

Going down the path and on to Mail Court, neither of them saw anything out of the ordinary. "Let's get from behind these buildings," Fish said, not wanting to keep walking behind the buildings. Every time they came to a corner of a building, he felt like somebody was around the corner waiting.

"Come on," Shed said, and they went down the Court and out the front of it and on to Griffin Street, where they continued on more at ease. Angling across the parking lot and passing under the shelter, they saw that nobody was out except for kids playing and headed towards the store at the front of the projects.

"It's dead as shit," Fish said, as they made their way across the field towards the store.

"True," Shed stated, really not liking it. It was as if everybody in the hood knew that something was about to go down and was staying in so as not to catch a stray. True, it was a couple of minutes after ten, but it was a Saturday and money was always coming through the hood. They hadn't even seen a crack-head.

"Ain't no cops or anything out, what's up?" Fish asked, mainly because he wanted to see if Shed knew something that he didn't.

"I 'on't know," She replied, and they made the rest of the walk to the store in silence.

Going in the store, Fish looked down the right side of the store where the video-machines were at and didn't see anybody playing on the six games.

"What can I help you with?" Mrs. Andrews, the owner, asked

"I need a pack of blunts," Shed replied.

"And let me get a Snapple and a box of Lemonheads," Fish replied.

"Yeah, let me get a Snickers too," Shed stated, knowing that he was going to have the munchies afterwards.

"No chips?" she asked, as she rose to go and fill their orders.

"Doritos?" Shed asked Fish, as he heard cars pull in outside and turned to look towards the door, but couldn't see whose ride it was.

"Cool with me," Fish replied, and went over to the Mrs. Pacman machine and took a quarter out of his pocket as the sound of multiple car-doors closing reached them. Looking at Shed, he said "who's dat?"

"I 'on't know," Shed replied, and started to go and look when he saw two policeman fill the doorway and come in. "Po' po," he said, and nonchalantly turned back around, while taking the money out of his pocket.

"Don't move!" the lead officer said, pointing at Shed.

"Who me?" Shed innocently asked, hand momentarily frozen. Under normal circumstances, he would have taken off, but the store only had one way in and one way out so his options were sorely limited.

Hearing the officer, Fish thought about tossing his gun behind the machine, but as soon as the thought entered his mind than the officer was coming into the store.

"Yes," the first-officer replied, quickly crowding Shed in case he had a gun in hand. "Put your hands right there on the counter," he said, as his partner came in behind him and Shed turned to put his hands on the counter, while looking at Fish with a worried expression. Seeing the second-officer turn and look in his direction, Fish turned back to the screen.

"Andre' Jones," the second officer said, coming towards Fish.

"Who?" Fish asked, acting like the officer didn't just say his name.

"Are you Andre' Jones?" the officer asked, coming to stand beside Fish. "And don't bother lying, you're only going to make matters worse son."

"Why you wanna know?" Fish replied, while still navigating Mrs. Pac-man around the screen.

"Because you're under arrest," the officer replied, and put a hand on Fish's shoulder.

"For what?" Fish asked, now releasing the controls and trying to turn, but the force of his grip held him in place.

"Malicious wounding, attempted murder, and possession of a firearm," the officer replied. "I'm going to need you to put your hands on the machine for me."

"Lookie here," the first-officer said, who was in the process of patting Shed down, but stopped when he found the gun. "He has a gun," he happily stated.

"Fuck," Shed stated, and looked towards Fish, who he knew had one on him as well. Hopefully not the one that he had used to shoot Danny Boy.

"Son, do you have a gun on you?" the officer asked Fish, who had turned to put his hands on the machine.

"Yeah," Fish replied. "It's on my waist," he added, his head drooping as he heard his mother telling him not to take the .45 out of the house this morning.

"You have the right to remain silent," the officer said, while reaching for Fish's waistband to get the gun.

Tawayne D. Love

Tear Drops On My Guitar

Tear Drops On My Guitar
CHAPTER 1

"He's a fucking dope-feign!" my mother screamed all up in my face. And when I say all up in my face that's exactly what I meant. Her finger was about a half an inch from my nose, which I knew from experience represented how close she was to smacking the taste out of my mouth. And if that wasn't enough of an indicator, of how pissed-off she was then her mahogany skin-tone was now tinged a serious red and her finger was dancing a jig right before my eyes.

Now I know you're wondering what had her that mad at me, though I'm sure you've surmised it had something to do with a man who was a dope-feign. Please allow me to take a pause in my recounting of this story to tie up some loose ends for you. It may make for a better story.

My name is Star Albright, and I'm a twenty-three-year-old sister from Charleston, West Virginia. I'm the color of a copper-penny, and would be considered thick but I don't have a butt. And to be thick a butt is a must. So, as they say, I'm a couple of Big Macs from being fat, but still cute to death. No, not beautiful, but cute. I have long jet-black hair that trails down to the middle of my back, along with full-breasts. Double-D size full breasts to be precise.

Now, the person she's calling a dope-feign is my man, Rich. He's twenty-six and we've been together for three-in-a-half years. And yes, I love his dirty-draws and all. Well...I do and I don't, but that's a whole different story. That would mean I'd have to get into Mecca, and now's not the time for that. Let's stick with Rich.

Though we've been together for three-in-a-half years, we've been messing around since right after I turned eighteen. He was, and still is, a fly-guy. Six-foot one-inches tall, high-yellow skin-tone and slim just like I like them. And oh, don't let me forget. He has some nice muscle definition to go along with that slim build. He prides himself on doing a hundred push-ups and two-hundred sit-ups every day. With waves swirling all over his head, along with dimples to die for, you're seeing the outer-picture of why I've played number two, three, and even four at times. And for those of you who don't know what, number four is, it's when you're introduced to other women as a man's cousin.

Anyway, three-in-a-half years ago I had a pregnancy scare. I thought I was pregnant and when I worked up the nerves to tell my mother she went postal on me. I'm still thankful that the only thing at hand when I told her was the ashtray because when she gets mad like that the first thing she does is look for a weapon. After she put me out, I called Rich and told him I was pregnant while my cousin Cerissa was taking me and my stuff to her apartment. He told me to meet him at his house, and when we got there him and his friend Kavah took my stuff out of the car and into the house while me and Cerissa stood there with dumb-looks on our faces. That wasn't what either of us was expecting, but come to find out he'd been secretly wanting a kid so I went from number three to number one just like that.

A few-weeks later, when my period came, I didn't have the nerves to tell him that I wasn't pregnant after all so I told him that I'd had a miscarriage. Instead of getting mad, or depressed, he said that was a warm-up for the real thing and we'd been living together ever since. That's why it was so hard for me to leave him. When I was down, he put me on his back until I could stand, and I felt like I owed him no less.

"I know," I sheepishly stated, though my eyes never left hers. I'd just asked her to loan me three-hundred dollars so I could pay the bills. She'd sarcastically said for me to get it from my man, and when I said, using the same sarcastic-tone, that he didn't have it, you would've thought she was a spry twenty instead of an over-weight forty the way she exploded out of the chair. "But he's my dope-feign and I'm a be there for him until he gets himself together like he was for me," I said.

"Unbelievably stupid," she stated, and exhaled a rush of breath that smelled like a pack of Basic menthols soaked in Old Milwaukee's Best laced with Epson Salt. Though the smell of it was noxious, her exhaling her frustration was a good thing.

"True," I stated, while nodding my head as she lowered her hand to her side and backed up some to sit back down. "But it's hard to turn your back on somebody that was there for you when you needed it."

"Somebody who's taking you down right along with him," she stated, and there for a fleeting second there was a look of sympathy on her face. Then it was gone and my mother was back. "Toughen up honey. I named you Star because you could reach it," she said, which was true. When the doctor smacked me, and I started crying, she said my crying was so musical that she named me Star so I'd always remember who, and what, I was. "Not so you could allow a no-account dim-wit to pull you down."

"His set-back's not cramping my style in the last," I said, which wasn't all the way true. It had really hurt my music. I'd been unable to write music for the club, but readily able to write sad-love songs since that's what I'd been feeling. Only when I thought about Mecca could I write songs tinged with love and hope.

Liar," she stated, and sat. "You'll be homeless, hungry, or both if I don't give you the money."

Raising an eyebrow, a smirk creasing my lips, I said "it's food in the fridge and my room's still empty."

Grinning, she said "when am I getting my money back?"

"I'll give you a hundred a week."

"I thought you only get paid every two-weeks?" she asked, and the look on her face let me know that she wasn't fishing either. Because of Rich, she was counting my pennies to ensure that I wasn't losing my mind and getting involved with drugs.

"Mecca's paying me to do the hook to his new song, and I'm doing a show at work next week and the week after that Cutty booked me to do one at."

"How much is Mecca paying you?" she asked, and I laughed. Mecca was locally famous, and had a nice following on the internet. His mix-tapes always did well, and some said that if J-Jerk hadn't been killed that Mecca would have been famous by now.

"Studio time and a hundred dollars," I replied. I was getting three-hours of studio time, plus the hundred dollars. The actual value was a thousand-dollars because three-hours of studio time with the head produce, Ivory the Coldest Rose, at the controls was nine-hundred dollars.

"Why is it that he doesn't have money to help you?" she asked, and I just regarded her like she was trying to bait me and I wasn't going for it.

"Momma, you know he's going through something right now," I replied, while shaking my head. "He's going to get it right though," I added, which was more like a silent-prayer to God for help. Today was the thirteenth and I owed three-hundred in over-due rent, the electric company was losing patience with me, and the water company would be shutting the water off any day now. And if I put the trash out behind the house, they'd bring it around and set it on the front porch right in front of the door so I had to put it in with one of the neighbors. We did have food though. I wasn't big on bumming meals so I made sure we kept food. I'd even taken his money for that, even though I didn't like doing that too often. I felt like if he kept a few dollars in his pocket he wouldn't have to do anything crazy if the urge to get high hit him.

Waving off what I'd just said, she said "keep working on your mix tape," while nodding her head in approval. "You need to spend more time with Ivory and less time at home. Hell, I doubt if he's there most of the time anyway," she stated, and for your information she was right. He wasn't. And at times, I was thankful because that let me work on my music in peace. But, when I started missing him I ended up getting my cousin Cerissa to ride me around to see if I could find him. Wasn't love a bitch?

CHAPTER 2

Stopping at Fas Check on my way home I spent two-hundred and seventy-four of the three-hundred dollars my mother had just given me on the electric and water bill. The rest I'd use for bus-fair around the city, though I had a ride to work already set up. Getting off of the bus, I walked the two-blocks to our house on Seventh Avenue down by the barbershop. Putting the key in the lock, I turned it, but saw that it the door was already unlocked and a sense of release washed over me. I hadn't seen Rich since last night around seven, and it was now a quarter to three so you know worry had been riding heavy on my mind. Going in and not seeing him in the living room, I hollered "I'm home," and tossed my handbag on the couch and locked the door.

"Rich, are you here?" I hollered. Not getting a reply, I figured he was in bed until I remembered that the door was unlocked. He always checked to make sure that the door and windows were locked before he laid down. He said that the streets made him paranoid like that. "Rich!" I hollered, as I made my way towards the kitchen. My worry-meter was now crossing sixty and about to jump to eighty because he hadn't replied.

Either he'd left and left the door unlocked, or he was in a dead-sleep. The other possibilities I didn't want to think about, but obviously, I was because my worry-meter was steadily climbing. Going down the short hallway off the kitchen to the bedroom and bathroom, no, sooner than I

126

was halfway down it I caught my first whiff of vomit and instantly knew that something was wrong. I knew enough about heroin to know that when it was good it made you throw up. Obviously, it had at least done that to him, and more than likely more because he wasn't replying.

Instinctively turning and heading back to the living room I snatched my phone off of the string of my purse and retraced my steps at light-speed. Well, not really, but it sure felt like it since I didn't run all that much. Turning down the hallway, I saw him sprawled out on the bathroom floor in a pool of vomit. From the signs of things, it looked like he must have been throwing up in the toilet and gotten dizzy and ended up on the floor where he continued throwing up until he passed out.

"Rich!" I exclaimed, and squatted over him to check his pulse. If he didn't have a pulse I was dialing nine-one-one, and if he did then I was calling Donita, his sister. Barely feeling a pulse, I changed my mind and started dialing nine-one-one, but stopped when my eyes fell on the needle off to the left, and a sob escaped my throat. He'd promised me that he'd never stoop to using a needle and there it was. The proof of our inevitable demise. Cerissa had made me promise that if he started using needles that I'd leave him.

Dialing Donita's number, I knew she was at work and prayed that she'd take the call. The last thing I wanted to do was call an ambulance, mainly because that would bring the police once they found out it was an over-dose. Just as the call was about to go to voice-mail, she answered and I exhaled in relief. "Hello."

"Nita, this is Star. It's Rich," I quickly stated.

Cutting me off, she said "what's wrong?"

"I think he's over-dosed," I replied around a sob.

"Bitch, suck it up. Now's not the time for crying," she quickly said. "Did you check to see if he was still alive."

"Barely," I replied, while fighting not to cry. This was way too much for me.

"Get him to a tub and run cold-water on him. I'm a call momma and get her over there. I'll be there in about twenty-minutes," she said. "But I need you to stay calm and keep it together," she added, and then hung-up before I could say anything. Taking a deep-breath, I felt like running my hands through my hair, screaming, and calling an ambulance at the same time, but instead I sat the phone on the sink and reached over to the tub and turned the cold water on. I needed to keep it together, and the only way to do that was to keep busy.

CHAPTER 3

It took about ten-minutes for Rich's mother, Mrs. Kay, to get there. Coming in she said, "How are you holding up?" as she continued towards the back.

"Fine," I nervously replied, while hurrying to shut and lock the door. "He's in the tub," I added, turning and hurrying to follow behind her.

Stopping at the entrance to the kitchen, she turned and stopped me dead in my tracks. I mean, she just abruptly stopped and turned. Had I been following right behind her I'd have probably had to move my head to the side to stop from kissing her it was that abrupt. "Go and sit in the living room. I'll take care of it from here", she stated.

"But," I started saying, and cut the rest of what I was going to say off when she started shaking her head. See, I knew she didn't like me all that much. At least I thought she didn't. And she was mean. I mean rattlesnake mean. At least to Rich she was. Me, I did everything possible to stay away from her so that's why I shut my mouth when she had that look on her face, followed by the slow shaking of her head.

"But you're going to wait in the living room until Donita gets here," she said as if she was finishing what I was going to say, and tilted her head in the direction of the living room. "When she comes tell her I need her back here," she said, and turned and continued on her way while I stood there for a full thirty-seconds with a dumb-look on my face before, finally turning and going back to the living room where I called Cerissa.

"Hey cuz, what's up with you?" she asked, when she took the call.

"I think Rich just over-dosed," I replied, and told her everything that had happened. Outside of a few "oh my God's," she listened and let me cry myself out. The only time I paused in the story was when Mrs. Kay came from the back and took all of the ice-trays out of the freezer and took them to the back.

"Star," she said, and paused. "It's time to leave. You've tried, but you can't save someone that doesn't want to be saved. He's gone."

"I know," I sadly stated, and looked at the television without really seeing it. "It's just hard. I love him," I said, and a vision of the old Rich came to mind. A fly-boy who was on top of his hustle when crack ruled the streets, but had turned into something altogether different when heroin had taken over.

"You love somebody who doesn't exist anymore," she said, as I heard footsteps on the.

"Donita's here. Let me call you back," I said.

"I'm already on my way over there. I'm downtown, so give me ten and I'll be there."

"Alright," I stated, and we exchanged good-byes as I stood and Donita knocked on the door. "Hold on," I said, and went to open the door.

Coming in, still dressed in her nurse's uniform she said "girl, are you alright?" as I stepped back and she caught the door on the back swing with a cuff and pushed it shut. She'd been a good friend since the first day I moved in, and our friendship had only grown. True, she was older than me by at least ten-years, but she was cool.

"No," I replied, my bottom-lip now trembling which caused her to grab me and draw me to her. "Donita, he's using a needle," I said, and broke down in her arms.

"No," she moaned while drawing me tighter against her.

"It was on the floor in the bathroom when I came in," I said, and I could feel her tremble slightly before she quickly collected herself. "Your mother wants you in the back."

Releasing me and taking a step back, she held me at arm's length and looked at me with a sad-look on her face. Rich was her youngest brother, and though she accepted the reality of the situation she still loved him. Especially since, she had practically raised him. "You know what this means don't you?" she asked, and I demurely nodded my head while lowering my eyes to the ground. Releasing me, she said "come on," and led the way to the back.

"She told me to stay out here," I said, which stopped her in mid-stride

Looking back over her shoulder, her features transformed to that determined, serious look.

"Now I'm telling you to come on," she said, and turned back around and continued.

Shrugging a shoulder, I followed her, while saying to myself "like mother like daughter." I could only imagine them two living in the same house together.

Going in the bathroom where Mrs. Kay sat on the toilet-lid, Donita said, "how's he doing?" There wasn't much room in there, but it was enough for me to peek around her and see him in the tub, naked, still out with the water up to his upper-chest with small pieces of ice-cube floating in it

"He's still alive," she replied, and then looked to me. "I thought I told you to stay in the living room?"

"I wanted to see how he was doing?" I teary-eyed replied.

"You should've known he was alive since I didn't come and tell you otherwise," she crassly replied.

"Leave her alone. I told her to come," Donita stated.

Looking from me to her, she said "she didn't need to see him like this."

"Yes she did," Donita stated, and the two of them locked in one of those stare-offs that I always lost. I could never understand the point of them so I rarely lasted long.

Finally looking back to me Mrs. Kay said, "then you need to learn how to do this because there might not be enough time for me to make it next time."

"I won't be here next time," I said in a low-voice, and my gaze lowered to the floor. Now didn't seem like the best time to be talking about something like that, but she was trying to teach me what to do in case it happened again. It might not have been the proper time, but it sure was the best. "I can't do this," I meekly added.

"You lasted longer than I ever could have," Donita sympathetically stated.

"Amen to that," Mrs. Kay stated, and for the first time in a long time she smiled at me.

"Do you know when he'll wake up?" I asked.

"Maybe in an hour or so," Mrs. Kay replied. "I'll stay until he's awake and on his feet and then I need to head home and get dinner started."

"Come on, let's go sit on the porch," Donita said after a last look at Rich.

"You can go up to Rite-Aid and get me a couple of bags of crushed ice," Mrs. Kay said, and Donita nodded her head in agreement and I backed out of the bathroom and lead the way to the living room with a heavy-heart. Even though I'd said what I just said, love was one of those crazy emotions that clouds the mind when a decision is made that's contrary to its nature.

CHAPTER 4

Rich was now in the shower. His mother, Donita, and Cerissa had all left, though Cerissa would be back in about twenty-minutes to get me and the rest of my stuff. I had already sent most of my clothes with her to take to my mothers, and was now getting the last of it together. I hadn't told Rich I was leaving yet, nor had he seen me packing. He had been covered in ice when I started, and I had quit once he came too. I felt like he should hear it directly from me instead of seeing me packing and figure it out like that. Finishing getting everything in the Nike bag, I took it to the living room and sat down and absent-mindedly watched television while he got dressed.

I wasn't looking forward to this conversation, but it was one that we had to have, so I figured I'd use the time to organize my thoughts and firm up my resolve. It took him about twenty-minutes to get dressed and come to the living room, and when he did, he had this chagrined, boyish, look on his face that was so cute that it almost melted my heart. I'd like to say that he knew he had messed up really, bad, but who knows. Who knew what was going through his mind right then.

"I know you're mad at me. I'm sorry," he said, as he came over and sat down beside of me and put his head on my shoulder.

Taking a deep-breath, mainly because I wanted time to stop the first thing that came to mind from coming out of my mouth, which wasn't I'm about to leave either, I said "Rich, do you love me?" and turned my head so he could see my face.

"No question," he replied, and lifted his head from my shoulder.

"Then why'd you try to kill yourself knowing it would crush me?" I asked. And for the first time I understood the meaning of a question, or statement, having the force of a punch. He leaned back from me with that wow-look on his face, and even blinked his eyes a few couple times as if the verbal-punch had clouded his mind.

"Huh, I mean," he stammered out before collecting himself. "It's not, I didn't," he said, before clamping his mouth shut and taking a deep breath. Looking away from me towards the television, he took another deep-breath and started to say something, but I cut him off.

"You can look at me when you say it," I said, which had the desired effect, though I can't really say that he was seeing me. He had that dazed look in his eyes, and I didn't know if it was a leftover effect of the drugs or the seriousness of the question.

"Star, you know it's not even like that," he said, trying to say it smoothly, but it came out all nervous. Even the smile was a wan-one. "I fucked-up. I know."

Cutting him off, I said "I'm leaving."

"No, no," he stated, eyes now wide, head shaking from side to side. "Come on Star, it's not that serious."

135

"I can't do it anymore," I said, my voice now full of emotions.

"I'm a get it together, I promise," he stated, while reaching for my hand.

"Like you promised you'd never use a needle?" I asked, and added "and don't bother lying. I saw it in the bathroom, along with the small trail of blood on your arm from it falling out. You lied to me Rich. You've been using it all along."

"Star...baby, I promise I'm a get it together," he said, off-balance now. It was as if his whole house of cards was crashing down around him.

"I can't do it," I stated, shaking my head as tears trailed down my cheeks and I released his hand. "I tried baby, but you wouldn't fight it. You just," I said, and trailed off.

"I'm a fight it, I promise," he stated, but the look on my face let him know that I wasn't buying it. "I'll go to rehab if you want. Come on baby, work with me," he pleaded.

"I've worked with you for four-months Rich," I said, pausing to choke back a sob. "I can't. Not anymore. You've got to do it on your own now," I said, and drew him to me and cried as he hesitantly wrapped his arms around me. While he held, me he tried talking to me, but I tuned out what he was saying and embraced the pain that came from the acceptance of our parting. Only in embracing it could I accept it. To do otherwise would be to walk away looking over my shoulder, and I didn't want to do that. I loved him, but I loved me more. He was choosing heroin over me, and as much as it hurt, I had to accept the choice. If for no other reason than for my peace mind.

CHAPTER 5

I spent the rest of Tuesday, and all day Wednesday hiding from everybody. Even myself. More than likely next week I would be at Cerissa's because my mother was getting on my last nerves, and then some. But for I was seeking refuge in home to come to grips with my new reality. And to do that I needed momma's love no matter how erk-some she was. Add to that that I knew Rich wouldn't come over here looking for me and this was where I needed to be. On a side-note he did call and text me all day Tuesday and Wednesday though.

Another benefit of being back home was that I had momma to helped me with my music. She wasn't that good at writing, but she was the bomb when at being a singing coach. And since I only had three-hours in the studio, I needed to get every note right so I could record as many tracks as possible. And with Ivory handling everything herself, I knew I would have to be at the top of my game. She wouldn't settle for less.

She had sent me ten-beats to choose from, and I chose all ten. I had written so many songs that I had a song for every beat. I had two, with about twenty left over. I knew I would never get to record them all in three-hours, but I aimed to do as many as I could.

"Hey hoe," Cerissa said, as she came in my bedroom where I was putting the finishing touches on my make-up.

"Next to you I'm a nun," I said, with a sly-grin as I looked at her through the mirror on my makeshift vanity table.

"I used to think you couldn't turn a hoe into a house-wife until Rich flipped you," she said, and I busted out laughing as she sat smiling from ear to ear.

"I'm a get you for that one," I said, and went back to putting on my blush.

"I'm just saying," she said, now grinning.

"Are you taking me to work?"

"I can if you want me to," she replied, as the grin transformed to a searching-look. I knew what she was thinking. Why was I asking her to take me to work when I already had a ride lined up? She had to think that the question had something to do with Rich. "What's going on?"

"Nothing," I replied, which was partway true. "Rich hasn't called all day."

"And that's bothering you why?" she asked, while putting serious emphasis on the "why."

"In two-days he called and text me over eight-hundred times."

"You counted them, didn't you?" she accusingly asked, while pointing a finger at me. "Bitch don't start lying. I know you did."

Rolling my eyes, I said "eight-hundred and seventy-three to be exact. And for your information I didn't answer any of them."

"It's the hoe in you," she said, and rolled her eyes.

"Last time I checked I'm the one that seems to keep a man, while you, Ms. Thing, seem to keep a jump-off," I said, while looking my face over to make sure that I had applied the blush evenly.

"That's one of the luxuries of chasing money instead of love," she said, and I had to turn and look at her on that one. "What?" she asked, after about a second of me looking at her with a raised eyebrow.

"What's going on with Rich?" I asked, and a smile broke-out on her face and she happily clapped her hands while laughing.

"I knew you'd ask," she replied, and a rueful-grin creased my lips. She threw the bait out there and I happily bit. "Well, everybody knew he od'd. Word on the street is that it was E-Neal's and every feign chased him down to cop."

"Go figure," I stated, while rolling my eyes. That blew my mind about dope-feigns. If your heroin almost killed somebody then everybody wanted it. Id-de-ot-tic to the max.

"Anyway, I checked a few of his usual places and he hasn't been around," she said and then paused. "And for you I tried finding out the tea."

"Nosey ass," I said, with a half-grin.

"Figured you'd want to know," she said, as my cell phone vibrated beside me. "Doesn't mean he's not using. It just means he's not out."

"They could be bringing it to him," I said, and picked the phone-up.

"True," she stated, while I looked at the number and saw that it was Mecca's. "And, before you ask no I didn't check to find out if anybody was."

"Hold on," I stated, and took the call on speakerphone. And no, it wasn't intentional. I didn't have my earpiece in. "Hey Mecca," I sweetly stated.

"What's up song bird?" he asked, which caused Cerissa to look at me with a raised-eyebrow.

"Bitch, let me find out," she mouthed to me, and I rolled my eyes in response.

"Getting ready to go to work," I replied. "What's up with you?"

"Seeing what's your plans for tomorrow night," he replied.

"Working," I replied. "I'm on the evening shift, and if I can I'm a coming to your show," I added.

He was doing a show at The Maze, which was going to be sold out. People were coming from Beckley, Huntington, and Logan to see him. That's how popular he was.

"Wanna do the show with me?" he asked, and I was momentarily taken back. And Cerissa's mouth fell open in shock.

"Well, yeah," I hesitantly replied.

"Good, good," he stated, in an upbeat tone. "I wanna do the Power of P, and you know I'm a need you for that."

Smiling, I said, "leave it up to you to want to do that song."

The Power of P was named The Power of Pussy. It was a street-ballad about what hustlers did for pussy. From caking a broad up, to losing his mind over it, to killing for it, it danced from one theme to the next with me serenading the hook. I even somewhat rapped the last verse of it, though it was more of a background to Mecca's lead. It wasn't my favorite song that we had done, but everybody that heard it loved it. Ivory had even come up with a better beat for it so he decided to release it on his next mix-tape.

"Club-bangers, street-bangers, and classics. That's what it's all about," he stated, which was his motto. "And this one could do it," he said, referring to The Power of P being a classic. "Plus, it's time for the city to really see you put it down. It's over with for that secret squirrel shit. If you're ready to do your mix-tapes then you're going to have to shine before the masses."

"Motivation," I prettily stated. "But I don't get off until eleven. I can be there by eleven-thirty, and ready by fifteen-till."

"That's what I'm talking about," he eagerly stated, his eagerness now in his tone. "You tryin to do some other shows with me?"

"Why are you asking crazy questions and you know I need the money?" I asked. "And how are we going to do this because I need you on two of my songs Sunday."

"I'm there," he replied.

"I know that, but."

Cutting me off, he said "I didn't say, but did I?"

"No," I hesitantly replied.

142

"Then leave it at that. Send me what you've got and I'll have something ready by Sunday. You should've been done said something, but I got you," he said. Who was I to look a gift-horse in the mouth? "We gone do our thing and get this money alright?"

"Alright," I happily replied, his mood infectious.

"I'll see you tomorrow night then," he stated.

"Bye-bye," I stated, and he reciprocated and I hung-up.

"Hoe, let me find out that pussy's back on the market?" Cerissa all but hollered, her joking tone completely gone. Instead, she had a surprised, somewhat impressed, look on her face.

"It's not even like that with us," I said, though my cheeks were tinted a bit. "Anyway, you were saying about Rich?" I asked, trying to change the subject.

"Spill it bitch," she stated, while waving my question away with a flick of her wrist. "And don't forget the explanation of why I'm just now finding out either," she added.

"Music," I stated, not knowing what else to say. "You heard the conversation. There's nothing going on but music."

"He's rapping with you for free," she stated.

"And I'm singing the hooks on his tracks for free," I stated, and then added, "well, not for free. He's giving me a hundred-dollars and paying for three-hours in the studio so I can work on my mix-tape."

"How much is an hour in the studio?"

143

"With Ivory three-hundred dollars," I sheepishly replied, and her eyes went wide in shock.

"Damn," she stated, and I couldn't help but smile. I loved her ghetto-ass. "That's a thousand-dollars, and you haven't even given him the pussy."

"I told you it's not like that."

Rolling her eyes, she said "try again."

"It's not. I swear."

"And your cheeks are red for no reason, right?" she asked, and I blushed even redder. "I'll tell you what, I'll ask him tomorrow night."

"You better not!" I exclaimed before I could catch myself.

Busting out laughing, she said "watch-out Charleston. Stella's definitely got her groove back."

CHAPTER 6

As Cerissa parked in front of Hooter's I grabbed my jacket from the backseat and said, "are you going out tonight?"

"More than likely," she replied. "What, you wanna go?"

"I need a break from the house," I replied, not wanting to be cooped up in the house tonight. The Hooter's in Charleston was turned up. And I mean turned up! Especially from Thursday to Saturday. There were a lot of men that came because of the twenty-two beautiful women that worked there, along with a cute me. So, after a nights work it was only natural for us to keep the party going and head to the club. That is those of us that were single, which I was.

"Call me when you're ready to get off and I'll let you know," she said.

"I'll talk to you later," I said, and picked my carry-case up from between my legs and opened the door and got out. And no sooner than the sound of the door shutting ended than I heard a car-door opening from the parking lot and I looked over and saw Rich getting out of the car. And yah boy was dressed to impress in some all-white slacks with the matching shirt, fitted visor and loafers. He even had his customary toothpick in the side of his mouth. Dope-feign he didn't look like. Shutting the door, he just stood there looking at me, waiting on me to come to him.

"There goes trouble," Cerissa said from inside of the car. "You need me?"

"No, I'm alright," I replied, still maintaining eye contact with him. I knew what he was doing, but I wasn't biting. He wanted me to come to him. Not today. I wasn't budging.

"Can I holla at you?" he finally asked.

"Yes," I replied, not moving.

"Walk with me," he said and nodded towards the street.

"Hold on," I said, and opened the door to set my things back inside. "Are you going to wait?" I asked Cerissa. "Wouldn't miss this for the word," she replied, all smiles. Leaning down some so she could see Rich, she said "hi Rich."

"What's up Risa," he said, and started over as I put my things back in the car and shut the door.

"I'm doing alright and you?" she asked.

"Just getting' my mojo back."

"Shine baby boy, shine," she playfully stated, and I couldn't help rolling my eyes. She was such a traitor.

Shutting the door, I said "come on," and walked down the sidewalk as he met me at the end of the car and we walked together to the end of the sidewalk.

"So, it's like that?" he asked, as we turned on the sidewalk and continued.

"Like what?" I asked, while looking over at him. I didn't have a clue what he was talking about.

"Like you iggin' me," he replied, and I mentally exhaled. "I've been blowing you up and you haven't gotten back at me."

Stopping and facing him, I said "Rich, we talked before I left. I told you I needed some space."

"That's not what you said, but I wasn't trying to hear that either," he said. Now that statement caused me to raise my eyebrow and look at him with a questioning look. I wasn't trying to hear that, a bit taken aback. Well, alrighty then.

"Excuse me?" I asked, sure he was playing or something.

"I'm fucked up and you just gone ride out on me?" he asked, ignoring my question. "On a nigga like me who held you down when you were fucked up," he added.

Pointing a finger that used to be manicured at him, I said "you're fucked up because you decided to get high on your own supply. And no matter what me or anybody else said, you wouldn't listen. You were doing Rich. And the hell with Star's feelings, hopes and dreams."

"I just said I fucked up," he stated, a hardedge now in his tone as his face-hardened up. A tone that had never been directed at me before.

"No, what you just tried to do was make your fuck-up my fault when you've been pulling me down the whole time," I said, and poked him in the chest. I didn't know who he thought he was talking to, but he had the wrong one and he knew it. There wasn't anything timid about me.

"Down?" he asked, and looked at me like I was tripping.

Taking a deep-breath, I gathered my frayed emotions back in and exhaled frustration. "Rich, you promised you would never use a needle."

Cutting me off, he said "and I swore I'd never do it again."

"I don't believe you," I said. "But what you should've said was that you were going to quit. You almost died for crying out loud."

"You really haven't read any of my texts, or listening to my messages," he said, though it was more of a question. And there was a hint of a shocked undertone in his statement. There was also a bit of uneasiness in it as well.

"No, I haven't," I replied, while shaking my head. "I'm hurting enough without adding fuel to my pain."

"Don't leave me," he stated, and took my hand in his and tried to kiss it, but I pulled it back once I saw what he was trying to do.

"You left me," I stated, and took a step back while crossing my arms. My mind and heart were at war, and his nearness was causing a lot of mixed signals to fly throughout my body. But I had promised myself that I was going to extract myself from this situation and I was sticking to my guns.

"I'm done baby," he said, and tried to smile, but only managed a wan one that told me that he didn't believe it himself. "It's over," he added, while stepping forward. "I almost died. I'm a go to rehab and get my mind right."

"That's a start," I stated, though I didn't believe him one bit. He just didn't look sincere at all.

"What else do I need to do?" he asked, trying to be all sexy.

"Get a job," I replied, a half-grin creasing my lips. Rich with a job didn't even sound right. The one time he was on probation his Probation Officer tried to make him get one and he found someone that would let him pay them to say he was working there. That was the closest I had ever seen him come to getting a job.

"Getting' money's always going to be my job," he said, that slick-grin on his face that always melted me.

"You'll relapse," I said with certainty.

"This is me Star," he said, and took both of my hands in his. "You already know once I set my mind to something it's done," he said and released my hands and reached in his pocket and took a knot of money out. As he held it to the side, I looked at it and had to admit I was impressed. And when he started counting through it, I was stunned. He counted out a thousand dollars in twenties, fifties, and hundreds, and what he had left was still twice as thick as the thousand-dollars he had just counted out.

"Where did you get that from?" I suspiciously asked. What I really wanted to know was who he had robbed.

"I'm a hustler," he replied, putting the money in my hand. "Take care of your music."

"Rich," I said, uncertainty now in my tone. Uncertainty that wouldn't let me close my hands around the money. "I'm done until I know for sure you've quit so don't be giving me this money thinking I'm coming home because I'm not."

"I'm done," he said, and pressed the money into my hand a bit firmer. "So you can come back home now. I'm back. I'm 'bout this money."

"No," I stated, and took another step back, while lifting my other hand to stop him from pressing up on me. And the strangest thing happened. His face turned ugly. I mean real ugly.

"I made you a muthafuckin super-star and this is how you repay me?" he asked, though it came out more as an angry hiss. Forcing my hand out of the way he pointed a finger at me and said "bitch, I picked you up when you was a nothin-ass hoe fuckin so you could chief for free. And now a nigga down on his luck and you gone vamp on me?" he spat.

I was so shocked that I couldn't even move, more less answer the question. "I ought to smack the shit out of you," he stated, and started to draw back his hand and do just that, but Cerissa's words stopped his forward momentum.

"Put yah hands on my blood and I'm a act a fool," she said, which caused Mock to look over his shoulder, while I looked around him, and we both saw her standing with her hand in her purse.

"It's cool," he stated taking a step-back and looked at me.

"I don't even know you anymore," I said, while slightly shaking my head.

Taking a deep-breath, he said "I love you, and just thinking about losing you got me all fucked up," and then turned and headed back towards whoever's car he was driving.

Letting Rich walk pass her, Cerissa came over and said "what happened?"

"I think he's losing his mind," I replied. That wasn't Rich. Outside of someone playing with his money, I had never seen him get mad until now. Had Cerissa not been here there was no doubt in my mind that he would have put his hands on me.

"Junky," she stated, a mean-look now on her face as we watched him walk pass his car towards Cerissa's. "What the fuck is he doing?" she asked, and went from zero to sixty on the walking meter back towards her car. Coming behind her, I saw him walk over to the open passenger window and toss the thousand-dollars inside. "What was that?" she asked loud enough for the people coming out of the restaurant to stop and look at her like they were looking at an angry black woman. Like she was about to put on a show and they didn't know whether to run back inside or watch.

"Her money for the studio," he replied.

And it was then that everything fell into place. He knew that I would be in the studio with Mecca all day Sunday, and that Mecca would be paying for it. When I had first told him about it a few weeks ago, it hadn't set too well with him, but what could he do? He didn't have the money, and he wasn't worried about Mecca taking me from him so he shrugged it off and agreed. Now, everything had changed and he was worried. At least that's what I thought. Had I knew that Mecca had posted on his time-line about me doing the show with him at The Maze, as well as putting up a picture of me on his Instagram page telling everybody the same thing, then I would have understood. Rich was in panic-mode.

"Rich," I stated, and he raised his arms up, palms out, which stopped what I was about to say.

"No string attached. Just make your music," he said, and then turned and headed to the car.

"What's up?"Cerissa asked, and all I could do was smile. There was momma's three-hundred dollars, along with the money to start my dreams. "Bitch, you're crazy," she stated, and smiled right along with me. I guess she was thinking what I was because both of our faces were lit up.

CHAPTER 7

Going outside for one of my fifteen-minute breaks so I could call Donita and talk to her about what had happened earlier between me and Rich, I turned my phone on and saw that I only had one text-message. Now I'll be honest with you I was kind of shocked. I had expected Rich to blow my phone up trying to make amends for what had happened earlier. Checking the message I saw it was from a number I didn't know and opened it. "I'm some shit. I know.

I don't know what came over me and I know sorry won't even cut it. I'm shook. I feel like I died already. Like somebody else is living in my body. I need you. I need you to help me find me again. I'm scared of what will happen without you. Like without you I have nothing but that. Please don't leave me. I really, really need you."

After reading it, for the longest ten-seconds I just stood there and looked at the message. A lot was going through my mind. I honestly didn't see myself able to go through what I had been through the last couple of months again. Add to that his actions earlier and I was fast approaching the point where I didn't even want to be anywhere near him. But I too had to recognize the reality of the situation as well. He was fast approaching the edge, and it might be that I was the only one that could bring him back. Or, at least keep him from jumping.

Shaking my head at the craziness of my life, I started walking towards the sidewalk and dialed Donita's number. Knowing her, she would definitely have some useful advice. She was really good at doing that.

"Hey girl," she said when she answered my call. "I hear you had some excitement at work today."

"Charleston," I stated, while slowly shaking my head.

"Bitch, you know these hoes can't keep their mouths shut," she said. I was wondering who the hoe was that had told her. I knew she really didn't like Cerissa, and as far as Cerissa was concerned, the feeling was mutual so she wasn't the one.

"I know," I said, "but let me tell you what really happened," I said, and told her everything that had happened. Even the message that he had just sent me.

"I really feel sorry for you," she stated, which wasn't what I was expecting. "I know you love him, and he knows it too. But I don't see any good coming from this."

"What if he stops using?"

"And when that happens what if he starts again?" she replied. "Or what if he says he's stopped, but really didn't?"

"I can't go through what I've been through again," I replied, really having no answer for that.

"Then get on with your life, or force him to get his shit together," she stated. "That is if you still love him."

"I do, but not enough to drive myself crazy," I said. "Been there done that."

"Then live," she stated, which was the obvious solution. "Do your shows with Mecca bitch, and shine like the star that you are."

"How'd you know about that?" I asked, wondering how she knew I would be performing with Mecca.

"You do know it's the twenty-first century right?" she replied, and laughed. "Bitch, you need to check your page and Instagram every once in a while. You're social media famous."

"Did Mecca put something up about it?" I asked, figuring that was what had happened.

"On both," she replied, and that's when everything fell into place. "Donita, I know why he's trippin."

"Who, Mecca?" she asked.

"No, Rich," I replied. "He thinks Mecca likes me and doesn't want me to leave him for Mecca."

"Doesn't Mecca have a woman?" she thoughtfully asked, and we both paused to recall if Mecca actually had one.

"I don't know," I replied, really not knowing. "I heard he was messing with Brianna."

"That's definitely not his woman," she stated, and we both laughed. I won't get into Brianna's history, but suffice it to say that even though she was beautiful her reputation for being head of the sack-chasers had ruined her chances of catching a serious man. She had dropped from head of the wifey-list to head jump-off. She was a sign that men were starting to smarten up and not wife pretty women with good twats who wanted nothing but their paper. She was currently what she should have been. Someone's jump-off.

"What have you heard?" I asked, knowing she had heard something. Though she was thirty-eight, she stayed tuned to the goings on of women my age. Happens when you have daughters a few years younger than me.

"Nothing definite, but I'll ask Channel and see what she knows," she replied. "But if he wants you bitch you need to get taken. That boy's going somewhere and with your singing you can go right along with him."

"With the money Rich gave me I should probably finish my mix-tape next week," I said, really not wanting to comment on that. And not just with her either. I liked Mecca. I think it was more of a crush than anything else. We'd never talked about anything significant, even though he had told me time and time again that Rich was holding me back. That my mother knew what she knew when she named me, but I was allowing a has-been ass nigga to hold me down.

"I know I better be the first to listen to it," she happily stated. "And I'm going to be at your show tomorrow night. I haven't heard the song you two are going to do, but he put a sample of it on his page and I'm loving it."

"You'll love it," I stated, figuring that from how beautiful she was she had used the power of pussy on hustlers to get what she wanted. "Let me get off of here. I need to call your brother."

"If I was you I'd wait until tomorrow to do that. You sound down enough already," she said, which was true.

156

"I think you're right," I stated, and we exchanged good-byes and hung-up. Boy, sometimes life was a good love song. Hot passionate love, followed by trials and tribulations, and then on to the break-up. The only thing left to decide was if this love song would end with a permanent break-up, or if we would be having that hot, passionate make-up

CHAPTER 8

"No breakfast?" I asked my mother as I came into the kitchen where she sat humming while watching The Price is Right.

"It's almost noon," she replied, and then nodded towards the microwave. "Sausage and bacon's in the microwave. You can make your own eggs."

"Thanks," I stated. Taking the three-hundred dollars out of my pocket, I sat it in front of her and went to make me a cup of coffee.

"What's this?" she asked, and I heard the bills make that distinctive crinkle sound as she picked them up.

"The money you loaned me," I replied, and picked up a coffee-cup.

"All of it?" she asked, while counting it.

"Yes."

"I thought you said you put most of it on the bills?" she asked, as she finished counting it.

"I did, but Rich met me at work yesterday and gave me a thousand dollars so I could finish my mix-tape," I replied, and that was rewarded with one of those huh's that conveyed displeasure as well as surprise.

"I wanna to ask how and why, but I'm scared of the answer," she said, while fingering the bills.

Finishing pouring the cup of coffee, I said "he wants me to come back."

Dropping the bills back on the table as if they had all of a sudden caught fire, she said "I want to say over my dead body, but I'm not ready to die yet."

Rolling my eyes, I said "I didn't actually take it. I told him no, but he tossed it in Cerissa's car when he was leaving. And, for your information, no I'm not going back. While he decides what he's going to do with himself I'm going to focus on me."

"What if he gets himself together?" she inquisitively asked.

"Then I'll think about it," I replied, which we both knew meant that I'd more likely be going back. That is if something better hadn't already come along by then. And we all know who that something better was right?

"Even if he does you should leave him alone and focus on you," she stated, and shook her head.

"But I'll think better of him if he does. I had to admit he was a good young man until he lost his way. Right now though, even with the money, he's shit in my eyes."

"Momma, I'm not going to sit around pining over him. I did that while I was with him. I'm going to focus on me and my music."

Nodding her head in agreement, she said "good." Motioning to the money in front of her she said "you can use this and pay me back later."

"Are you sure?"

Nodding her head in reply, she said "go ahead before I change my mind and get to thinking about what I can do with it at bingo tonight."

"Thanks," I said, and picked the money up. "I'll be back to make my breakfast. I've got something I need to take care of real quick."

"How many eggs do you want?" she asked, as I turned to head out of the kitchen, back to my bedroom.

"Two," I replied, and went to my bedroom and sat on the bed and took my cell phone from the charger. Going to Rich's message from last night I hit the callback button. I'd wanted to reply to the message, but I didn't want to send my reply to a number I didn't know. I'm sure my business was already all over the city, but why invite more, huh?

"Took you long enough to call me back," I heard a chipper Rich say on the other end of the line.

"I wasn't going to call," I said. "I can't believe you."

"I'm not trying to lose you," he said, and that caused me to exhale through pursed-lips.

"You sure could've fooled me," I said. "When are you going to rehab?"

"I was talking to momma about it the night you left me," he replied. "If you'd of listened or read any of my messages then you'd of known."

"Why didn't you talk to Donita about it?" I asked. I felt like she was a better person to talk to about that than his mother. Or maybe it was because I knew Donita better.

"Because she's not talking to me."

"I'll talk to her and let her know what you wanna talk to her about and see if she'll help you."

"Fuck her!" he exclaimed. "She thinks I'm supposed to kiss her uppity ass or something."

"Rich, I'm not coming back home until you quit."

"I quit," he said with emphasis. And I could detect a hint of an attitude in his tone.

"You can't quit using heroin like that and you know it," I said, adding just as much attitude in my tone as he had in his. "Quit acting like you just started using yesterday," I stated. He must have thought I was stupid.

"We're not even going to do this," he said.

"You're right because I didn't call to argue with you. I called to let you know that I'm not coming home until you quit. And if you take too long then I'm moving on with my life," I said. "And that's really more than you deserve after what you said yesterday. You really hurt my feelings."

"That wasn't even me," he said, his tone now remorseful. "Droppin' Felicia to be with you was the best decision I ever made."

"Actually, you didn't just drop her," I said, smiling. She went from number one to number two, and once she realized that she couldn't get her spot back she had too much pride to be his second-woman and bounced. "You can cut that out."

"Once she saw you was wifey she was out," he said, and laughed. "I fucks with you and you know it. Hold me down,

I'm a get it together. Word, I'm a get it together. But I need you. I need you to get back right."

"You need help Rich," I sadly stated, a feeling deep within me telling me that he really didn't want to get any help, and without it nothing would change. Without help, this would be nothing but a reoccurring cycle.

"You're the help I need."

"Alright, well let me get off of here," I said. This was going nowhere. I'd said what I called to say. Now the ball was in his court. If he didn't get any help, I was gone. Point blank, plain and simple.

"You're not going to invite me to the show?" he asked, which made me smile. Here we go with this.

"Right now what I really need is some space so I can think," I replied. "And what you need is to focus on getting some help."

"Damn, it's like that?" he asked, the remorseful-tone now gone. Replaced by an angry one.

"Yes," I replied. "Me, you and heroin can't be together. I'm going to focus on my singing and you need to focus on getting some help."

"You gone get one of these bitch-ass niggas fucked up," he stated, and hung-up.

Blowing air through pursed-lips, I looked to the ceiling and shook my head. Lowering my head I sent Donita a text explaining to her that Rich was talking to his mother about getting some help, but could she get with him and see if he was really serious? Putting the phone back on the charger, I stood and started towards the door, but stopped when it started vibrating on the charger. Going back, I picked it up I saw that it was a text from her and opened it.

"I'm calling him now. I'll take him today if he's serious, but he's full of shit. Girl, focus on your music and forget about him."

CHAPTER 9

Getting ready for work, I packed my make-up kit so I would be able to get ready for the show after work. True, I might need it at work tonight, but my Compacc would more than likely take care of that. Going to the closet to get my guitar I stood before the open door with a dumb-look on my face. I'd placed it right there on the left side of the closet, which is where I always put it so it would be out of the way of my shoes. And now it was gone. Turning and hurrying to the living room where momma was at, I said "momma, have you seen my guitar?"

"You didn't tell Rich to come and get it?" she asked.

"Huh?" I asked with a surprised, mixed and confused, look on my face.

"While you were gone Rich came. He said you sent him to get it to re-string it for your show tonight," she replied, and my jaw came unhinged. "You did send him, didn't you?"

"No," I replied, while shaking my head in wonderment, trying to figure out what type of game he was playing.

"I'll be damn," she stated, throwing her hands in the air. "What the hell would he do something like that for?"

"Because he knows I don't like performing without it," I replied, and turned to hurry back to my room to call him.

That guitar had been my sweet sixteen present from my mother. No, it wasn't new. It had actually been in the family for a long time. It was my aunt Florence's, but she ended up

164

going insane when I was nine. For whatever reason my mother had given it to me, and since Aunt Florence was my favorite aunt, I had readily accepted it. Now it had become like a psychic crutch to me. I even used it when I was in the studio.

"Well kiss my ass!" she exclaimed, as I ran towards my room and she rose to follow me, though by the time she made it I had the phone in hand and was hitting the send-button.

"What's up baby girl," I heard Rich say, followed by the sound of a guitar string being plucked.

"Rich, what type of game are you playing?" I asked in exasperation. "Why'd you come and get my guitar for?"

"It needed to be re-strung," he replied, and laughed.

"You're high," I stated, noting that his voice was sounding real groggy-like.

"How you gone try to leave me for that fuck-nigga?" he asked.

"What are you talking about?"

"It better be bringing that guitar back," my mother hollered loud enough for him to hear.

"Tell Mrs. Kay I said I'm sorry for lying to her," he said.

"You can tell her when you bring it back," I stated.

"I'm at the crib," he said, and hung-up on me.

Seeing me lower the phone and look at the screen, momma said "what did he say?"

"I have to go to his house and get it," I replied.

165

"You kids trip me out," she stated, while rolling her eyes and then turning and leaving.

Trip her out, I said to myself, wondering how she could fall for that trick? She didn't even like Rich, I said to myself and went to finish packing, and then waited for Emily to come. Yes, I tried making sense out of all of this, but it was hard. How did you make sense out of a ball of confusion? Something wasn't adding up to me.

I'd never given Rich the impression that I liked Mecca. My crush on Mecca was something I had kept to myself until Cerissa heard the conversation between us yesterday. Somehow I just kept running into the idea that she was saying stuff she wasn't supposed too, but that just didn't sound like Cuz. When Emily came, I put my stuff in the back of the car and said, "Em, can you swing around to Rich's so I can get my guitar please?"

"Sure," she replied in her Arabic accent, which somehow made the one-word sound exotic. And no, I wasn't into girls, it was just something about the way she talked that caught everyone's attention. Even those who knew her. She made every word sound exotic. Sending Mecca a text, I asked him if him and Rich had had a run-in? I needed to know if they had because, if so then the only person that could have said something about me and him would have been Cerissa. A few seconds later, my phone was ringing.

"I thought you were done with that fuck nigga?" was the first words out of his mouth.

"It's complicated," was my reply to that. "But have the two of you had a run-in?"

"The day after you split on 'em our paths crossed and I let 'em know he'd blown a good thing for a bag of poison," he jokingly replied, and even I had to smile. "He said a couple of things and I said a couple of things and that was that. Wasn't nothing serious though. Why, what's up?"

"I was just wondering where he got the idea that I was leaving him for you," I replied.

"Because I tole 'em his loss was my come-up," he replied, and laughed. Now I won't lie I almost had the sheepish-girly grin on my face when what he said sunk in. Probably the only reason I didn't was because Emily was probably bird-dogging my every word.

"Mecca, I'm flattered that you think that way about me. I really am, but what you said is complicating my life and I don't need that right now," I said, though my tone conveyed more than I wanted it to. He couldn't help but hear the pleasure in my tone. I was really flattered.

"What, are you going back to that?" he asked in disbelief. "Come on Star, quit shittin' on yourself."

"It's complicated," I replied, which was the best answer I could give under the circumstance. "Please, let me uncomplicated it myself."

"Cool, if you promise to put the music first."

"I'm putting me first," I said with conviction.

"That's good enough for me," he stated. "I'll see you tonight then."

"Tonight," I stated, and we exchanged good-byes and I hung up.

"You and Rich aren't together anymore?" Emily asked before my phone was in my lap. Nosey-ass, I said to myself.

"No," I replied. "I need to focus on me and getting me together," I said. It felt like I was spouting a party line or something every time someone asked that question.

"Sounds like Mecca wants to focus on you," she said, and smiled. "I definitely wouldn't mind him focusing on me. That is if you don't want him."

"Come to the show tonight and I'll let him know," I said with a sincere look on my face. I would do absolutely nothing of the kind, but she didn't need to know that.

CHAPTER 10

As soon as the car was in park, I said "I'll be right back," and reached for the door-handle.

"Alright," Emily said, as I opened the door and got out. Shutting the door, I headed to the house through a fence that had no gate. The outer-yard was like a resemblance of our relationship. Three-fourths of a fence, with no gate, and a driveway with no fence. And put simply the yard needed to be replanted. Way too many cookouts and parties in the six-years that Rich had lived here, and now the grass was showing the effects of its mistreatment. Potholes here and there, as well as stains in the grass.

Going up the steps to the porch, I saw that the door was slightly ajar. Just as I was about to reach for the knob I heard the faint sounds of a guitar playing and paused. That was weird. Rich didn't play the guitar. He was one of the most musically uninclined people I'd ever met. Opening the door, I saw that he wasn't in the living room and looked towards the kitchen, figuring that he was more than likely in the bedroom. As my eyes moved towards the opening to the kitchen, they passed over the entertainment center, which was to the right of the entrance. Normally there were three-pictures on top of it. One of me, one of him, and one of us in the middle of the two, but they were all gone. In their place was a piece of paper that called me as surely as the flame calls a moth.

169

Shutting the door, I went to the paper and, for some reason I couldn't explain, I didn't pick it up. All I can say is that it didn't want to be touched, which it communicated to me on a subconscious-level. Placing my hands to either side of it, I leaned down some and read:

Star:

I can remember being locked-up in the Regional that time for a few days. You never knew it, but I wrote you a few letters while I was there. I never sent them because, at the end of the day, I knew I was lying. See way back then I knew I was gone. See, it's hard to put into words that feeling of that diesel running through your veins. It's like the best orgasm ever, multiplied by ten. I thought I could manage.

Stay on my square, but I fell off. Then I thought I could get back up, but that dragon kept spewing poison at me to make me chase it. Rehab ain't gone work, and losing you ain't either.

I'm fucked-up and I don't know what I'm a do. I got back on my square, but I'm off it again. Now I'm sittin' here with a gun

and I don't know who to kill, myself or that bitch ass-nigga. But, like he said, he's capitalizing off my mistake. So, I can't be mad at him. The letter was longer, but that was as far as I made it before all of these strange, dark, images started running through my mind. All of them with him back there dead.

"Rich!" I hollered, and took off at a dead-run to the back, sparing a glance in the bathroom to make sure that he wasn't in there. Going in the bedroom, I saw my guitar-case, with another piece of paper on top of it, but no Rich. Looking around, a worried-look now on my face that only seemed to heighten when it dawned on me that the sound of the guitar playing was coming from inside of the closet. About to head in that direction, my eyes were drawn to the note on the guitar case.

"I Choose You," it read, but I only took note of it in passing. The closet wasn't that big to begin with, and definitely not big, enough for him to be up in it playing a guitar with the door shut.

Yanking the door open, eyes now wide, face taunt with trepidation, the look turned to one of confusion when I saw that the closet was empty except for my guitar that had a CD-player behind it emitting the sounds of a beginner playing a guitar. Seeing a white envelope in the back of the strings, I picked the guitar up with one hand and took the envelope out with the other. Hurrying to the bed, I sat and put the guitar in my lap, and took the paper out of the envelope and opened it. If you're reading this then it means that you still love yah boy, which means that what I'm now doing isn't for nothing. You're probably wondering why my clothes aren't in the closet. Well Big Sis is checking me into a serious rehab where I'll be at for 90-days. I know my word is some shit with you, but you can call her and find out. We're on our way there now. The thought of almost losing you woke me up, and gave me the strength to buck that

Dragon spewing poison at me. Believe in me and know that I love you!

By the time, I made it to the middle of it I was crying. He was really getting some help was all I kept saying to myself over and over. Fear and trepidation had turned to confusion, and from confusion to joy as I wore the biggest smile I'd ever wore as my tears of joy trailed down my face, making soft thumping sounds as they landed on my guitar.

1 Am

I Am

CHAPTER 1

SASHA

I am Sasha Fierce. At least I am when I'm at West Virginia University, where I go to school at. When I'm at home in boring old Charleston, West Virginia, I'm plain old Sasha Jones. And since I was on my way to Charleston for two-weeks of my summer vacation I guess I was about to be boring old Sasha Jones.

I had two-weeks to turn up before I started my summer job as an intern at Alcorn, Cobbs, & Frederick's, which was an accounting firm in Harrisburg, Pennsylvania. And yes, I was a bean counter. Next year I would have my accounting degree, and shortly after that, I would start studying for the test. I wanted to become a Certified Public Accountant, which wasn't easy. It was easier to become a lawyer than it was to become a CPA.

"I don't know why we're not staying up here for the summer," Bre, my best friend and sometimes lover, said as she put the bag in the trunk. She was from Philly, and really didn't like Charleston all that much. Her number one knock against it was that I wasn't openly into women there. Here, I was a thrill-seeker, that's why I'd inherited the name Sasha

Fierce. Well, that wasn't the only reason. Me and Beyoncé kind of look alike. The only real difference was that I didn't have the mole, and I was a true red-bone, though the term second-generation mulatto fit me better. And for those of you who were visualizing Bee without the mole and the skin-tone of a red-bone don't. She has more tits and hips than I do, even though my butt-cheeks are fatter.

"Because I'll be stuck in Hagerstown all summer, and I wanna go home and hang out for a couple of weeks," I replied, while she was leaned over making sure that all our stuff was situated in the trunk. And for good-measure, I smacked her on her petite cheeks. I loved a fine man and a beautiful woman. Honey-brown skin-tone, with hair the color of her skin, and some full C-cups that she loved to keep on display. She was definitely beautiful. Around five-six and a hundred and five-pounds, she was definitely put together just right. But, like me, her body wasn't her main attraction. With almond-shaped eyes, as if the Indian in her had come out in her eyes, and lips that were made for kissing, she was even more beautiful than I me.

"Keep it up," she stated, leaning back up and reaching for me. Quickly dancing out of her reach, I said "hurry up so we can go," and headed to the opened passenger-door. It was a two-in-a-half our ride home and I planned on sleeping the whole way.

CHAPTER 2

JET-LIFE:

Got to be kiddin' me, I said to myself as I recounted the seventy-five hundred dollars that I had just been given by Red, my little homey from city park who was pulling off. He had just given me the money that he owed me for some raw that I had fronted him, but he had the nerves to short me five-hundred. This was only seventy-five hundred and he was pulling off like everything was alright.

"What's wrong?" Brittany asked from the driver's seat of my '13 Cadillac Escalade. She had been with me long enough to know when something was wrong. I was staring daggers at the back of Red's Mustang with hate in my eyes so she knew that something was up.

See, I was between a rock and a hard-place. Everybody knew that I was caked up, and I had an image to protect. An image that I had cultivated myself. I spent most every day in a pair of Robbins that cost at least a thousand dollars. And that was just for the jeans. The shirt and hat were always with the jeans, and add a pair of fresh-kicks to it and at some point and time every day I had on an outfit that cost at least fifteen-hundred. And we're not talking two or three of them in the stash either.

I had twenty-such hook-ups so there was no doubt I was about that life. And the Escalade was so cold that when I was in Cincinnati where I was at when I wasn't in

Charleston, Bengals players were checking for it. Smoke-gray, with TV's everywhere and some bang that commanded attention, it was like that. And I'm not even going to tell you about the shoes on its feet. Sweet, that's all I'm a say. Floating old school on the spinners that lit up and made it look like the rims were made of diamonds at nighttime.

"Count this and make sure it's seventy-five," I replied, and handed her the money while picking my phone up with the other hand. Since I was clean, I wasn't tripping on being in South Charleston like this. Had I been dirty I would have caught up with him later on. You didn't play around in South Charleston when you were dirty.

"What did he to, short you?" she asked, taking the money while I started texting him.

"That's what he thought," I replied, and sent him a text telling him to hit me right back. "I need that nickel. That's my drinkin' money," I added.

"Are you going to Diamond Cut's part tonight?" she asked. Diamond Cut, one of the local DJ's, was throwing a party tonight, which was called Bitches Night Out.

"I got reservations for VIP, but I don't know if I'm a be there," I replied. Word on the streets was that she was throwing it for the lesbians and bi-crowd, but Diamond Cut's parties were always packed so I was hedging my bets. She wasn't gay so I knew regular hoes were going to be there just because it was her party. And if I let the hood know I was coming then everybody would come just because. Yeah, I got down like that.

"How much was VIP?" she asked, as my phone vibrated and I saw that it was a text from Red.

"Fifteen," I replied, and opened his text. Without reading it, I sent him one back telling him that I said to call me.

"It's only seventy-five," she stated, and folded the money up to put in her purse. "If you go who are you going with, JRoot?"

"No question," I replied. "Twin and Dog gone probably ride too. What, are you doing?" I asked, figuring that she was with all of the questions she was asking.

"More than likely," she replied.

Seeing that I had another text message from him, I opened it and saw "Why?" No the fuck he didn't, I said to myself, now feeling like punching him in the motherfuckin mouth. Dialing his number, I put the phone on speakerphone and turned the truck on.

"What up?" he asked upon answering the phone.

"Turn around," I replied.

"Why?" he asked, his tone hardening up a bit.

"Because I said so," I barked at him, my tone full of the authority of my position in these streets.

"Because the last time I checked I don't work for you nigga. Now turn that shit around," I all but hollered. "And the last time I checked I don't work for nigga. Now turn that shit around, " I all but hollered.

"I was just sayin."

"That you're on your way back, right?" I said, cutting him off. Fuck what he was saying. I wasn't trying to hear any of that.

"Yeah, yeah, yeah," he quickly replied, and added "give me five."

Hanging up without saying anything else, I looked out of the window with that intense look I got when I was pissed. I hated it when these niggas played with me. Like I was a joke and wouldn't lay any of them down.

"Calm down," Brittany said, reaching over and taking my hand in hers.

Gently squeezing her hand, I said "you got that," and took another deep breath. I hated when niggas made me look cheap. "Remind me to cut 'em off next week."

"Monday," she said, while nodding her head as I looked over at her with a half-grin.

"What's up?" I asked, smiling.

"Freaky-ass," she replied, knowing exactly what I was getting at. "What happened, your lil' African bunny wasn't enough for you last night?" she asked with a raised eyebrow. She knew what I was on last night because she had dropped me off over her crib. Yeah, chicks like Brittany were definitely hard to find. They loved to play their role.

"She's not you," I replied, and, ever so slowly, looked her badass from her head to her toes.

"And don't you ever forget it," she stated, and leaned over and gave me a searing kiss. Good thing for her I'd brushed and flossed this morning since she didn't go both ways or she would have had her first taste of pussy.

CHAPTER 3

SASHA:

I love coming into Charleston from the direction of Morgantown. It seems like forever there's nothing but mountains and fields and then all of a sudden you come around this big mountain hoping to see something other than the same ole' same ole and then there's Charleston. A City tucked in the valley of a chain of mountains. My city. And every time I come home, I feel invigorated. It may be that the long miserable drive's finally over, or it could be that I actually miss home at times, but the feeling never ceases to happen.

Because I wasn't staying at my mother's I had to direct Bre to my sister's house on the West Side hill. Chantel was twenty-five and had a good job as a receptionist at a law firm. She was living alone right now because her man had just been sentenced to five-years in the feds so I was taking advantage of her vulnerability.

Calling mom and letting her know that we'd made it home alright, we made it to Chantel's and I got the key that she left me under the swing and we went in and started unpacking.

"Are we going out?" Bre asked, while hanging our clothes up.

"More than likely," I replied, while putting the clothes in the dresser that I had just folded up. "There's supposed to be a big lesbian and bi-party that everyone's going to."

"And when were you going to tell me?" she asked, and I didn't have to turn around to see that she was staring daggers at me.

"When I made up my mind about going," I replied. Turning, I said "I don't go to those types of parties at school so I wasn't sure we were going here."

"Then why bring it up now?" she asked, her gaze tightening up some. Just by her stance, I knew she wanted to go. She was with going to parties like that, because she was openly bi-sexual.

"Because everyone's going," I replied, adding an indifferent shrug to my shoulder. "Diamond Cut's throwing it," I indifferently added.

"I remember her," she said. "I didn't know she was gay."

"She's not," I said, and smiled. The thought of her being gay was really funny. "She's just hosting and D.Jaying it. That's why everyone's talking about going."

"Why do you even go when you can't be you?" she asked, and rolling her eyes.

"Be me?" I asked, my tone letting her know that I didn't want to go there again. If she didn't want to respect the fact that I swung both ways then I would make sure that she got the point tonight.

"Sasha Fierce," she replied, which caused the smile to falter. That was like a body-shot right there. "Do you know what it's like watching you in the club, seeing how miserable you are."

"And for your information I'm not scared either," I stated. "When Malacca and Landra comes up to school I still do me," I said, not even bothering to speak on Kim and the other girls who went to WVU from Charleston. And that wasn't counting Lil' Lush and the guys who basically lived in Morgantown when school was in. They all knew how I tore the club down when I was in it.

"But when you're here you won't go near the dance floor," she said. "When the little girls be out there doing their thing, and I'm stuck on the sidelines watching with you all night looking dumb and pretty I be pissed."

"You get on my nerves," I stated, though there was affection in my tone. I knew what she was trying to do.

"Who are you?" she asked, the challenge to be me not only in her voice, but communicated by her body language as well.

"You're not slick," I replied, smiling, though my arms instinctively crossed my chest.

"You still haven't answered my question," she said, ignoring my statement.

Eyes lowering some, I felt the transformation come over me. Confidence infused my core, and exuded from every pore in my body. Sex appeal leaked from me as if I was Bee, as I said "I am Sasha Fierce."

CHAPTER 4

JET-LIFE:

"What up Unc," Lil' Lush said on the other end of the phone as I sat looking at the two 64' plasma TV's hanging from the ceiling on either side of the fireplace. Each with its own entertainment system beneath it.

"I was about to hit you up and see what was up for the night," I replied, and yawned. I'd laid down for like three-hours, but I was still tired as hell. I would've liked to have slept longer, but I had to go and meet Tish so I could make a run. I took broads on all of my runs because they had that secret pocket that the law never found the dope in. That was unless they brought a dog along.

"You haven't heard?" Lil' Lush asked, and whatever he was about to tell me had him amped up.

"What's up?" I asked, not even bothering to guess. This was Charleston. Lord knew what these niggas was getting up to.

"Word is Sasha's supposed to be putting her thing down at the party tonight," he replied, "And she's calling out all of the wanna be dancers in the city. She brought Bre from up the way, and they be reckin' shit."

"Who is she?" I asked, and reached for my iPad right beside of me, which was already on my Facebook page, so I could see what was going on. At first I'd thought she was a rapper or singer, or something, but he said she was calling out all of the dancers so I figured she was a dancer. And I couldn't think of a dancer named Sasha that would have him hyped like that.

"Remember the weekend before Christmas when you came up the way?" Lil' Lush asked, and that's when it clicked who he was talking about.

"Her," I replied, and grinned. Her and her girls had shut the dance floor down, and then disappeared into the night before I could get at her. "She 'bout to make it do what it does?" I asked.

"That's what Diamond just put up on her page," he replied.

"She got her girls with her?" I asked, as I began formulating how I was about to shit on the city tonight. I was in my body that I had left my 2013 750i in Cincinnati, along with my Hummer, but I did have my kitted out 2009 Mustang Shelby GT-H convertible that was blue, with the blacktop. And since I had the dual exhaust pipes, with the engine super-suped up, it would growl out loud and command a gang of attention.

"Bre," he replied. "And she's bad as a muthafucka. Even badder than Sasha on the real. What's up though? We gone shut shit down or what? Say the word and I'm a break out the Stingray and we gone make it happen," he said, and that cinched it. I definitely had to take the Shelby. He had the 2017 Stingray Convertible, with the chameleon-coat paint job. And for rims, he laced it with the new Giovanni's.

"You gone finally show it in the city?" I asked, now getting amped. He never drove it in Charleston. The closet it made it to Charleston was Beckley when he took the turn off to go around Charleston on his way to Morgantown from Charlotte.

"I was bringing it out next week for the roof-top party anyway," he replied. Now that was supposed to be the party of the year, and it was only May. Someone had rented out the rooftop of the old Job Corp building and was throwing a party up there. It only had two requirements to get in. Tickets were a hundred and fifty-dollars apiece, or five-thousand to get in VIP, and you had to be wearing all white. If you had anything other than white, and your white wasn't crispy clean, you would be out front chillin.

"I'm a go in a all-white stretch Hummer limo," I said, not wanting to take any of my cars. With A.P bringing his Aston from Huntington, and Lil' Lush now bringing the Stingray, I was cool. The stretch-Hummer limo I was getting in Cincinnati was enough.

"Yo, we gone be live. You know Root gone stunt," he said, and that was more than likely true, even though he did it with old school rides. His baby was his white on white SS 5.0L 1989 Monte' Carlo. I had to admit he had that boy right though.

"Aye yo, let me get up off of here and hit 'em up. I'm at the spot by the Park so when you get a minute swing through. I gotta move to make, but give me an hour and swing through."

"Bet it up" he stated, and hung up.

Dialing JRoot's number, I put the phone to my ear while going on Leeshia Lee's page to see what was going on. If it was crunked over there then I would have to add my comments to the post and get shit really hyped. I didn't know why she didn't send me a message letting me know what was going on in the first place. Didn't nobody get the city turned up like I did. I got this bitch crunk!

CHAPTER 5

-*KUTTA:*

"There's something big going on in Charleston tonight," my girl, Savannah, said as she came in the bedroom carrying an armload of t-shirts and boxers.

"What's up?" I sleepily asked, as my gaze travelled the length of her athletic body, which was totally opposite to mines. I was a big boy. 5' 7" tall, and around 280 lbs. Yeah, I loved to get it in, so what?

"Remember Sasha?" she asked, as she went to the dresser where she was stacking my essentials together for my week long stay in Charleston, which was forty-five minutes away from my home town of Huntington, where I would be doing a video and finishing my mix-tape at..

"That dancer broad that goes to the U," I replied. We had crossed paths a couple of times, and I had tried to get her and her girls to dance at my shows in Morgantown or do a video with me, but she had always played me to the left. And I'm not going to get into how she carried me when I tried to bust her down.

Nodding her head, she said "her and her girls are supposed to be dancing at the party I was telling you Diamond Cut's was having. It's trending," she stated, which got my attention. Not much of shit trended in West Virginia.

Getting my phone from the nightstand, I hit Diamond Cut's up. I was going to call her anyway to let her know I was sliding through her party later, but now I wanted to be a part of it. Shit, it was trending. You could never have your face attached to too much in this business.

"I guess this party just went from a bitches night out to stuntin galore," she said upon answering my call.

"You know this," I said, smiling. "I don't even know how you put this shit together without hittin yah boy up anyway."

"I really didn't put it together," she said, which kind of struck me as odd. True, it wasn't her party, but as host and D.J, it was hers to put together. "I didn't even know Sasha was dancing until she tagged it to my page. And Jet Life had already put the thousand dollars up for the winner when he called to ask me what was up."

"Damn," I stated, mainly because I needed a second to figure out how I was going to be a part of all of this. "Tell you what, shit, let's do it right then. I'm a put two more stacks with his, and the winner gets a lead-spot in my video next month."

Whistling, she said "you niggas are way too much. Why don't you and Jerk perform?"

"He won't be back from Charlotte until late," I replied. "He's down there doing a show."

"Then you do it," she stated.

Laughing, I said "I thought you would never ask."

"Send me what you're going to do and let me get up off of here so I can get the word out on what's going on," she said.

"Alight, I'm a get up," I stated, and we exchanged good-byes and hung up.

"You really went over the top on that one," Savannah said, while looking at me and shaking her head. "That's something the two of you should have put out there and let marinate for a week or two before the party."

"True, but fuck it, I couldn't turn down the opportunity anyway," I said, while going on to my Facebook page to post what was going on, and hype up Sasha's challenge. Shit, we was about to do this shit way too big.

CHAPTER 7

-KUTTA:

"Let me hit that," I said to my man Tip, who I had known most of my life. At present, we were riding to Charleston, and this nigga was hogging the shit out of the blunt.

"Damn, can't a nigga get right. Roll your own," Tip replied, which caused S-K to laugh from the back seat.

"Ole' winey-ass nigga," S-K said in his gruff tone. A tone that transitioned on to a track hard as a muthafucka. Him and Tip were coming up because they were on two of my tracks, though we had two more carloads of niggas, with another carload of bitches bringing up the rear. Jerk's video was tomorrow and we were stuntin for Hun hard as a bitch.

"Pass the muthafuckin blunt," I stated, already gone off the first two-blunts of that apple diesel we were puffing.

"Bra, with lips like that you might wanna let that nigga have it," S-K said, and I looked at Tips lips and fell out laughing. That nigga had lips like that nigga from Fat Albert. What was his name, Rudy? I think that's him, with them dumb big ass lips.

"Yo, that was fucked up," I said, still laughing. I was so gone that even corny shit like that was funny as hell.

"Fuck yah'll niggas," Tip said, while exhaling a cloud of smoke.

"Dog, you've chiefed like half that shit already," S-K said, which was true. When Tip fired up a blunt he tried to take as much of it to the head as possible before passing it. But since it was his weed we were smoking, I wasn't tripping.

"Pass that shit," I said, and reached for the blunt as my phone started ringing.

"Here," Tip stated, and took another big ass pull before passing it while I looked to see who was calling me.

Jet-Life, I said to myself as I took the blunt from him and put it to my lips. Taking a quick hit of the blunt, I took the call and said "what's up my nigga? What it do?"

"This money," Jet-Life replied, which was his motto. If ever there was a nigga about his money I had to admit that it was him. True, he was a kingpin trick, but he was about his gwap as well. "Word is you gone be in the city tonight at the party?" he asked. Yeah, yeah, yeah, I knew where this was coming from, but I just played along. Diamond must have put him down with my move and he was calling to fill me out on it.

"I'm a be up that bitch for like the whole week," I replied. "I'm in the studio and doing the video with Jerk. I know you gone be there," I said. Shit, from what I was hearing the whole muthafuckin Charleston was going to be in the 'Page reppin' that nigga. My nigga Jerk was going broke on this video because it was an underground classic. Shit, on the real, I was honored to even be on it with him, even though I was deeper in the game than he was. Music was my life, while this shit was a hobby for this nigga. But every time he dropped something, which was like four or five singles a year, it went dummy all over the internet.

"You know I don't fuck with them West Side niggas," Jet-Life said, and I fell out laughing on his ass.

"Nigga, get off of that dumb ass shit," I said, still laughing. "That East Side, West Side, shit's for niggas with no money. Niggas getting' to that bag ain't got no time for that shit. Nigga grow up," I said, still laughing him out.

"Them niggas don't like us cause we got that bag," he said, and I shook my head at that.

"Preach," somebody said in the background on his end.

"Who that?" I asked, moving on. I didn't have no time to waste even on a forty-five minute ride.

"Lil' Lush," he replied.

"Tell my nigga I said what's up," I said, and took a hit of the blunt while he relayed my message.

"He said what's good," he said, coming back on the line. "Word is you doing something big at the party," he said, his tone switching to that searching tone.

"Yeah, we gone bring the hoes and see what they can do. Sasha called out all of the dancers so I figured we'd make it official. Shit, you had a stack on it so I figured we'd really go dummy in that bitch tonight," I replied.

"We gone do that my nigga," he said, his tone amp'd up. "Now the whole city gone be in that bitch my nigga. That shit gone be off of the wall."

"Hun gone be deep in that bitch to," I said. "Shit we like four-loads deep on the way up there now."

"Where you stayin'?" he asked, and added "you know you can rock with me if you need it. Shit, I don't be up in this bitch like that anyway."

"I got a spot at the Embassy already on deck," I replied. "You know when I'm in my element I be needin' that peace and quiet to get it in and ain't no peace and quiet around Jet Life," I jokingly stated.

"Nigga you always turned up."

"Turned up, knob broke," he stated. And that's pretty much how he lived every day.

"You bringin' my girl along?" he asked, referring to that Molly. I kept that shit on deck like niggas kept weed.

"You ain't even gotta ask that dumb ass question," I replied. "Ain't a spot I'm in that she ain't. What's up though?"

"I'm a meet you at the telly," he replied, and I grinned. "I'm a need one."

"Bet it up," I stated, and we exchanged good byes and hung it. Shit, that was an ounce sale right there.

CHAPTER 8

SASHA:

We all decided to do our finishing touches at Malacca's house, though the decision was made more by default than anything. She was the only one with her own place, and my sister was already getting on my nerves. When she came in the house, the first thing out of her mouth was that me and Bree wasn't sleeping in the same bed together. I just rolled my eyes and flippantly asked her how was her day at work?

So now, we were at Malacca's, and we were all basically done. I'd decided to wear an all-white True Religion jeans outfit, with True Religion wrote in cursive letters across the back of the jacket and the front of the shirt in blue. And on my feet, I had a pair of all-white Randy Moss Asics on because running shoes were good for dancing, and I loved me some moss.

"You're really going to do it," Landra said, smiling at me as I helped Bree finish getting her hair together.

"She is Sasha Fierce," Malacca said while rolling her eyes as she finished with her lipstick.

"And don't you ever forget it," I said, while cutting my eyes to her. I knew she couldn't stand me when I was Sasha Fierce because that was the only time she wasn't in control of the group. That's when I was. The confidence I exuded was to intoxicating even for her, even though she was twice as beautiful as I was. My beauty compared to hers was like comparing Beyonce to Stacey Dash's. Bee was beautiful, don't get me wrong, but everyone knew that Stacey Dash was something else altogether different.

"Especially if you lose," Malacca jokingly stated, while recapping her lip-gloss.

"Beta's don't lose," Bree stated, and left it at that. She couldn't stand Malacca, but always played nice for me.

"God yah'll make me wish I would've went to college," Landra wistfully stated.

"Cut it out," Malacca said to Landra.

Rolling her eyes at Malacca while hitting her with a dismissive flick of her wrist, Landra said "are we going to the 'Cage first or straight downtown?"

"The Cage," I replied, knowing Malacca wouldn't like it that I'd just made the decision, even though that's where she would have chosen anyway. "And when I go back to school in August you can come up and stay with me if you don't have to work."

"For real?" Landra asked, her shock mixed with happiness on her face and in her tone.

"Definitely," I replied. I had pointedly not made the same offer to Malacca to let her know her place. I couldn't believe she would even jokingly insinuate that we wasn't going to win. K-Kutta could keep his video appearance, but I needed that three-thousand dollars. Me and Bree were going to have a ball with that in Harrisburg.

"What are we going to do with this money you're about to win?" Malacca asked.

"Sash, didn't she just say something about us losing?" Bree asked.

"Sure sounded like it to me," I replied.

"Oh get off of it," Malacca stated, rolling her eyes. "Everybody knows you're going to win so what we wanna know is what are we going to do with the money?" she asked, while looking at me. I think she knew better than to ask that question to Bre.

"We are doing absolutely nothing with my half," Bre replied, which caused Landra to smile as she looked at Malacca to see what she had to say.

"Are you dancing?" I innocently asked, and both Landra and Bre busted out laughing.

CHAPTER 9

JET-LIFE:

We were killing it so much that I'm not even going to describe it to you because I know the haters are going to think that there was no way that some country boys from West Virginia was killing it like that. Just let it be known that I wasn't the only one Robbin'd out though. Lil Lush had shot to the crib and came back screaming money, and when JRoot showed up with his Robbin hook-up I knew tonight was going to be one of those nights that went down in history.

Looking at Lil' Lush's Stingray, which was reflecting the nighttime sky mixed with the street-lamps, I had to admit that nephew was killing it. That bitch was so sweet that even I had to whistle. "Nephew, I'm lettin' you know now I'm getting' that eighteen."

"Already ordered it," Lil' Lush said, grinning. Now you know I wanted to ask him what he had going on that let him drop close to a hundred for this one and order the next one, but I stayed in my lane. If he wanted to put me down with what he had going on then he would, but other than that, I would mind my business unless it came to me another way because he had something major going on that I needed to know about.

"Damn," Twin stated.

"Killin' it," Dog stated.

"Shit Mook, I was gone ride with you, but not tonight," JRoot jokingly stated.

"Whatever," I said, and hit the button on my alarm.

"He killed it Mook," Twin said, and I knew he was trying to rub it in. He knew I hated riding in someone else's shine, but it was all good. This was nephew, and I had something on deck for the summer that would put me right back at the head of the class. I was getting that '68 Shelby. And for those of you who don't keep up with cars I'm talking about that classic Shelby that was going for close to two-hundred.

Because we were rolling deep I texted K-Kutta to let him know that, I would pick the zone of molly up at the club. I was already going with a half, and ten Viagra's, so I could put that up for next week since I had another quarter in the crib for tomorrow night. That was unless tonight turned out to be one of those nights. Then I'd use all of that shit tonight, and the club would fuck around and turn into an orgy.

When we bent the corner of the side-street that the Bird Cage was on I was ready to bang "Clique," by Kanye, Jay, and Big Scan, but Lil' Lush turned on Fly Rich, by Rich Gang, Stevic J, Future, Tyga, and Meek Mill and killed it. He had some thunder in the back of that little muthafucka so I kept mines in reserve for the club. Yeah, mines was louder than his, but this was his moment. Let Charleston see his shine.

When we reached the club, we all parked with the front of our cars facing the road, except for Twin. He parked his

Benz how he wanted to. He was like Dog, an old head, and accepted in any hood so he didn't feel the need to be on point like we did. Me, JRoot, and Lil' Lush were in foreign territory so we carried it just like that even though it was only a couple of minutes after nine and there probably wasn't twenty people in the club.

Putting my top back up I got out and we headed inside, with JRoot leading the way. Now, for those of you who don't know what the Bird Cage is like it's the hood hole in the wall. It's super-small. If a hundred people were inside it was packed to capacity, that's how small it was. It's purpose of it to us was to get oiled up before hitting the regular club, even though us East Side niggas didn't come over here all that much. We usually got oiled up at The Empty Glass, but tonight was an exception. Sasha had posted that she was coming here so this is where we were going to jump it off.

Coming in I saw Big Taco sitting at his customary table in the corner by the back door and threw him the deuces, which he half-heartedly tossed back. He was still in his body at me over some nonsense that was going on back in Cincinnati, but it was all good. He'd get over it since I wasn't the one who did the choosing.

"What's up Unc?" I heard Lil' Lush say and followed his gaze to Bar, who was playing pool with his old-head partner Cutty from the Bottom.

"What up family," Bar said, a smile breaking out on his face as he looked at all of us.

"Chillin," Lil' Lush replied, as he went over and gave him some dap.

"Damn, it's gotta be somethin special to have yo ass out tonight," Dog said, following behind Lil' Lush.

"You know he's chasin'," Twin said.

"He's on his own," Cutty said, while pointing the pool-stick at Bar. "I tole you I wasn't lettin' you get me in the dog-house again."

"Shit, you got me in the dog-house the last time," Bar said, while dapping Lil' Lush up as we all laughed. These two and their wifey's. Why did hustlers still getting' money even wife women for? It was a recipe for destruction.

"Ya'll a trip," JRoot said, shaking his head, though he was smiling. "What's everybody drinking on?" he asked, and we all told him what we wanted.

Turning to Bar, I said "guess what?" getting amped a bit.

"What?" Bar asked, his eyebrows raised a bit.

"Nephew got the '17 Corvette Stingray," I said, pointing to Lil' Lush.

"Say word?" Bar asked, looking from me to LIl' Lush, which told me that he had really kept that close to the chest. Bar wasn't just his uncle, he had a presence out here in these streets. He was an O.G. hustler who'd put in his work and was respected for it so Lil' Lush keeping that from him let me know how close he was playing his cards.

"Lil' somethin I had in the cut," Lil' Lush replied, while adding a shrug of a shoulder.

"I'm with yah'll for the night," Bar stated, smiling. "Yah'll on somethin big."

"Legendary," I said, correcting him. "This shit's about to be legendary," I added.

"Hell no," Cutty said, while shaking his head. "You're not getting' me in the dog-house again," he said to Bar.

"We gone be together so it's cool," Bar said, both him and Dog now smiling.

"We were together the last time I was in the dog-house," Cutty said, a smirk now on his face to let Bar know that he wasn't buying that.

"I was there that time wasn't I?" Dog asked, looking from one to the other.

"You gone be there this time too," Bar said, and they all fell out laughing, and we joined them. This shit was about to be crazy.

CHAPTER 10

SASHA:

When we came in the Bird Cage there wasn't but about twenty people there, but we'd posted on our pages that we were on our way here so within twenty-minutes a nice little crowd had gathered.

"So you're just going to float through and not holler at me?" Lil' Lush asked, while standing behind me. Like every woman in Charleston and Morgantown, I used to have a crush on him. I say "used to" because Sasha Fierce had a crush on no one, but everyone had one on her, so when I turned to face him it was with the look of a woman and not a love-struck fool.

"I spoke to you when I came in," I sweetly replied.

"You didn't speak to me though," Jet Life said, and extended his hand to me "Jet Life," he stated, by way of introduction.

"Does that define your lifestyle or is that just a nickname?" I asked, while taking his hand and holding on to it. Yes, I remembered him. The only way a woman my age didn't know who he was, was if she was living in a convent or something. And he was like thirty something, but the life of every party he was at. When he put it up on social media that him and his crew were, going to a particular club that club was packed by the time he arrived. And he never had to pay to get in.

"I'm a lifelong member of the Mile-High Club," Jet Life replied. And I do have to give it to him the confident manner that he said it in had me leaning towards believing him. Reaching in his pocket he pulled out an unfolded rubber banded stack of money and said "what you think I keep ten-stacks on deck for at all times?"

"That's not really ten-thousand dollars," I said, now knowing that he was faking. Nobody just walked around with ten-thousand dollars in their pockets.

"She thinks I'm one of those fake-ones," he said to Lil' Lush. "Want me to bless her game?"

"Preach," Lil' Lush replied, and I'll admit that piqued my curiosity some. Was that really ten-thousand dollars? It sure didn't look like it.

"First thing you need to know about me is that I don't do no fakin'," he said, as he took the rubber bands off of the money. And when I glanced around most, everybody was watching. Even the guy who was putting money in the jukebox had stopped to watch. "I'm a hand 'em to you a thousand at a time, now watch," he said, and proceeded to count ten-thousand dollars in one-hundred dollar bills, only stopping at every thousand to hand them to me.

"You're crazy," I said, while looking down at the money in my hand.

"Let me know when you're ready to fly above the friendly skies," he said, grinning.

"I know drinks are on you tonight," I said, and I handed him the money back.

"I got you and your girls," he said, and put the rubber bands back on the money and then put it back in his pocket. Taking a fatter knot out of his other pocket he counted out ten twenties and handed them to me. "This is for yah'll."

"You're stuntin real hard," I said, taking the money from him.

"Hard enough that I'm a be posted up in VIP waitin on you to get tired so you can slide through and holla at me," he said, his meaning clear.

"Waiting on me?" I sexily asked, while batting my eyelashes.

"On you," he replied, his gaze boring into mines as the tip of his tongue parted his lips to moisten the top-one. As if he was getting them ready for a kiss.

CHAPTER 11

K-KUTTA:

It was about ten-thirty when we left the hotel and headed to the spot the party was at. And no, sooner than we turned on to the block the mall was on I saw that downtown was turned up. And the closer we got to the party the more people I saw. It was deep as shit down here. It was so deep that when we made it to the block the party was on we couldn't even turn on to that street. People were so deep that wasn't no traffic on that street, so we went around to the parking lot on Summer's Street by the old McDonalds and parked there and trooped back the three blocks back to the club.

Turning on to the block, I saw the line was most of the way down the block, and the club was on the other end. It was people everywhere just chillin, having long-sense gave up on getting in the club. I knew it was a lot of clubs down here, and it looked like everybody was either going to get in here or parking-lot pimp for the night.

As we made our way down the sidewalk, I had my three badass dancers in tow. Honey's bad, Arab, ass was definitely on my right arm, and Lucky's thick to death white ass was on my left. I always kept Kamari's light-skinned ass out front because she always cleared the way for yah boy. It seemed like dudes just wanted to let her through, and I filled the void of her passing.

As we made it to the front, I saw two-bouncers barring entrance to the door, with a guy sitting on a stool holding a clipboard. With all of these people out here, there was no way the spot was packed to capacity, but it had to be because they wasn't letting anybody in. From what I'd heard, this was a big restaurant that was converted to a club on Friday and Saturday nights. They usually only opened up one of the big ball-rooms in the back, but tonight they were opening both of them up, which meant that a lot of people were up in there. Exactly where yah boy needed to be.

"K-Kutta and sixteen," I said to the guy holding the clipboard. "Got you," he stated, while checking my name off of the list. "I'm a need you to check in with Diamond big man," he said.

"Got you," I said, and followed Kamari through the doors, and the sounds of "Break it Off," by Rihanna & Sean Paul, was playing, though at a lower-volume out here.

As we came in the restaurant part the bar took up most of the right-wall, and it was people packed up two and three deep waiting on drinks. They had like four or five bartenders back there and they were dumb-busy. The sitting area to my left wasn't packed though, but straight ahead at the door, a crowd of people were trying to get in back.

"This bitch is live," Wax said from behind me.

"It's so many white hoes up in this bitch," Snaks said, which caused Lucky to look over her shoulder at him.

"Really though, fat boy?" she said, and blessed him with a withering-glare before looking back forward and muttering "idiot."

Going to the back, we stalled out at the door because the hallway was super-packed. Whatever was going on back there had brought everything to a standstill so I told Snaks and Borris to clear us a path and five-minutes later we finally made it down the hallway to the club-part. When we came in

"Mercy" was playing and all we saw was a mass of gyrating bodies, and tables that were in the way because nobody was sitting down. And quite a few had a woman dancing on top of it. In my mind, I was hearing Deandre Jordan on that State Farm commercial saying they were "going down."

Pointing to my left Snaks and Borris fought us a path that way. This shit was stupid packed, and it was just now after eleven. Lucky for us the VIP was in that direction because my fat-ass was tired from all of the pushing to get through. It was there that I saw the roped off area that the dance contest would

be held in, along with Diamond Cut's DJ book and the table that the judges would sit at.

Getting everybody through VIP, I took Snaks with me and went to the bouncers at the roped off area and told them who I was and pointed to Diamond Cut and let them know I was going to holler at her.

Thankfully, they let me pass because I was in no shape to fight my way through the mass of bodies to get to her.

Seeing me coming, she blessed me with her beautiful smile, and a hug when I got there. Baby girl was like that, though I'd never hollered at her. She kept my music in rotation on Friday and

Saturday nights, even though I wasn't from Charleston, so I didn't wanna take a chance on messing that up.

"This is crazy," she hollered in my ear.

"You did this," I stated.

"Not this," she said, laughing as she lightly smacked me on the back. "You all did this."

"You should see outside. It's twice as many people trying to get in out there," I said.

"Oh my God," she stated. "This is going to be crazy. And Jet Life isn't even here yet."

"Damn," was all I could say. One thing about him, he had a way of getting a party all of the way turned up. And this one turned up any further would be crucial. Super crucial.

CHAPTER 12

SASHA:

When we made it to the club it was a little after eleven and the line was now all of the way around the corner. And it didn't seem to be moving. There was an audible groan from the almost thirty people that was with us. No one wanted to wait in that long-line. They came to party, not wait in a line for almost an hour to do so.

"Come on," I said, and led the way to the front of the line, though I stopped a couple of times to talk to people I knew who inevitably ended up getting out of line and coming with us. By the time, we reached the door I couldn't tell you how many of us it was. What I do know is that the line had shortened dramatically.

"Sasha Fierce," I said to the guy with the clipboard sitting down. "And my party," I added.

Smiling, he said "I didn't know your party had a hundred. I was thinking more along the lines of ten."

"Fifty," I quickly countered.

"You do want room to dance, right?" he asked, while raising an eyebrow. "Pick fifteen. The rest can wait."

Seeing that he wasn't going to budge I turned, ready to pick the fifteen when people began to holler Jet Life like they were chanting the Dahli Lama's name.

JET-LIFE

Coming through the crowd with my peoples in tow, I heard the last of what Bent, the owner, had just said to Sasha and said "how many can I pick?"

Looking to Jimmy, Brent said "let 'em in but cut 'em off at fifty."

"Alright," Jimmy said, and a resounding cheer went up from everybody that super-inflated my already inflated ego. Looking at Sasha, I saw that she was looking at me, and the look on her face said that I could get it. "You ready?" I asked, motioning to the door.

"Don't forget who you're waiting for," she replied, winked, and turned and led the way inside.

Got to love being me, I said to myself, knowing that I was hitting that tonight. When I was done with that, she was definitely going to be a life-long member of the Mile-High Club

CHAPTER 13

SASHA:

This was the first time I'd been here, mainly because, for the most part, it was a restaurant that catered to the young, hip crowd. And they were mostly white, or black wanna be's. But tonight the whole city was here, though not so much out front even though that would change. They were letting fifty more people in.

As we made our way to the back, I noticed most everybody starting to look at us. Since most of them didn't know who I was, I figured it was Jet Life they were looking at, though I saw some pointing at me. But after tonight most, everyone would know who I was. When I came to a club, everyone would know who Sasha Fierce was.

JET-LIFE:

When I came in, I made my way through the throng at the bar and gave Sallie, the bartender, five-hundred dollars and ten-grams of molly. Thinking better of it, I gave her two-thousand dollars because of all of the people here tonight. She knew what it was for, like most everyone else did. That was money for free drinks, and the molly was to lace drinks for those who wanted to ride. More than likely I was going to need the ounce from K-Kutta because there were so many people that it had to be a gang of sevens and above. And for your information you had to be a seven or above to get a free drink. Six and under needed to buy their own.

"Are you about to go crazy tonight?" she asked with that mischievous grin of hers.

Shaking my head in reply to her question, I said "ballistic." Everybody was going to be up in here stuntin, so me stuntin would be like doing the same thing they were doing. I was going down in history tonight. It took us about twenty-minutes of fighting through the crowd to actually make it to the VIP section. Even I was like woe. It looked like a mass of gyrating bodies dancing to "22" by Taylor Swift. I was wondering what Diamond Cut's was tripping on playing Taylor Swift until I remembered that she was a really big pop star now.

Seeing the roped off section, I spotted K-Kutta's people in VIP, and saw that Sasha's girls were sitting near them so we took a table in between them. Just as we started to sit down "My" by Future started to cut in on her song and I knew that Diamond Cut's had seen me coming in. See, I had this understanding with D.Jay's that when I came in they played this song for me. It had started out that way, but now it was something altogether different.

"Everybody, Jet-Life's up in the building," she said, as "22" was faded out and "My" was the only thing playing, and the crowd started hollering "Jet-Life" over and over as they continued to dance. Normally I would already be on the dance-floor getting it in, but I wanted to get us some seats. Once everyone outside realized that the only way they were getting in was to buy seats in VIP it would be packed as here to. Right now, it was just ballers here chillin' so it was still some empty tables.

Going to the rope, I looked over and saw K-Kutta, Sasha, and Diamond at the booth chillin and was ready to go. No sooner than I was out of VIP and on the dance-floor, I was mobbed by so many women that it was crazy. And you know me, wasn't no way they were going to shine on me. They got to tossing it and I was tossing it right back. Shit, they'd just have to hold off on getting the dance-contest started because it was going down.

CHAPTER 14

K-KUTTA:

When Jet Life came out of the VIP section I thought we were about to get started, but that was quickly deaded when he was mobbed by a gang of shorties. Within a matter of moments, it was like ten-rings of shorties around him, and he was getting it in. I knew he went hard-body in the club, but I never really watched him. I always had my own demonstrations going down, but I was now getting an up-close look at how he got in the club and he was making it do what it does. The next thing I knew his peoples were coming out of VIP and getting involved, and mines quickly followed, followed by most everyone else. Anybody else that was left in VIP wasn't much into dancing because that whole area was getting it in. And then I saw Sasha and her girl going across the roped off section and I smiled. This was going to be real.

Within three-songs, Jet-Life's shirt and hat were gone, and it was still going down. Looking at my watch I saw that it was twenty-eight minutes after eleven and knew that my midnight show was over, but it was all-good. Wasn't nobody leaving this party until the lights came on and the music stopped. It was going down all over this big ass room. As I looked out across the dance-floor, I was proud of the part I had in making this happen. The two-thousand invested in this was the best investment I could've made.

Diamond Cut's let it go on for like ten-songs before leaning over and saying, "I had to give 'em what they came for."

"True," I stated. They had come to party with Jet-Life and she had given them what they wanted. All of a sudden, a siren went off, followed by the sound of automatic-gunfire and the lights came on and everybody was looking around dazed, with that dumb expression on their faces that came from something unexpectedly distasteful happening. She'd shut the party down just like that.

"Alright everybody, yah'll know what we came for," Diamond Cut's said, and they tossed a bunch of catcalls and foul language at her for that. At that time, I really think they could have cared less about the dance-contest. They were in their elements. Nothing existed but the groove, and the person in front of them or around them. Shit, I even saw guys trying to dance with Jet-Life and I was giving them the benefit of the doubt that they wasn't gay, but who knows.

"We're going to take a twenty-minute break, and I'm going to need," she started saying before being cut off.

"Turn the muthafuckin music back on and shut the fuck up!" someone hollered.

"You're fuckin up the party!" someone else hollered.

Going on as if no one had said anything, Diamond Cut's said "I'm going to need those who entered to come up front and check in. As yah'll know Jet-Life has brought the first five-hundred people beers so go ahead and head out front and get a beer before they're all gone. That'll give everybody a minute to cool down before the party starts back up."

With those words, the grumbling stopped and you could see whole groups of people heading for the door, though still a lot stayed put and headed towards the empty tables.

"Yo, this shit's crazy," I said, smiling. "Bet you better not turn a song on in this bitch or it's back on and poppin'."

"Bet you I don't either," she said.

"Are you going back to VIP to hang out before everything gets started?" she asked. "If so tell the first waitress you see to send me something to drink up here."

"Got you," I said, and gave her some dap and a hug before heading back over to the VIP section. This was going to be crazy. For the first time I was feeling like the contest was fucking up the flow of the party.

CHAPTER 15

JET-LIFE:

She just killed the whole vibe, I said to myself, ready to storm over to Diamond Cut's and tell her to crank the party back up, but stopped myself. This shit was now all of the way in the way and the sooner we got it over with the quicker I could get back to getting my groove on.

Hugging a couple of the girls I was dancing with, I turned down quite a few invitations for them to come back to VIP with me. Sasha was there, and I was with the fellas so that was dead until after two. By then I would know what type of time she was on. If she was playing hard to get then I'd get me a duo for the night. Plus, I needed to get some more molly in my system. Outside of what I'd taken at the crib, I didn't have time to get right before I was mobbed.

Going back to our table, I saw that everybody was back including two more. Herm, one of my dogs from the Park was now there, and E-Neal, a East Sider that I really didn't like. "What's up my dude," I said, going over and giving Herm some dap. "Why didn't you let me know you was down with the movement. You know what it is," I said, as he stood up and gave me some dap.

"Damn, he ain't even gone front and play nice. He gone just cut me out right in my face," E-Neal jokingly said, which brought a few smiles from everyone.

"Damn, chill out. You know I'm a say what's up," I said, dapping Herm up. "But Killa Hill gotta get it first."

"Why is it that nobody's ever died up there?" E-Neal asked, looking at Dog.

"It ain't called Killa Hill for the bodies," JRoot replied.

"It's called Killa Hill because of the killas," Herm stated.

"Four of you are from Killa Hill and ain't not one of you got a body," E-Neal said, and both Dog and Bar busted out laughing.

"That you know about," I said, tired of him and ready to tell him to beat feet, but the waitress killed my train of thought.

"Do yah'll want anything," the waitress asked.

"Yeah, let me get a bottle of 'Roc," I replied, and everybody ordered a bottle. Giving her fifteen-hundred dollars, I said "take a fifty-dollar tip out of it and tell 'em to hold the rest. We're just getting' started. Keep that shit flowin'."

"Sure will," she said, smiling as she took the money.

"Now back to you," I said, and headed back to my seat. Fuck shaking that his hand.

"Nah, I'm just saying," E-Neal said, smiling from ear to ear. "Well, I see I made you mad Mook so I'll leave that alone."

"What the fuck did you come over here for anyway?" I asked. "I know you didn't come over here to get on my nerves."

"Nope," E-Neak replied, while shaking his head. Leaning forward some, he said "now I know you're still mad at me over Trish," and that did it. Both Bar and Twin erupted in laughter, while everyone else looked at us smiling because they didn't know the history.

"I'm a fuck you up," I said, dead-ass serious.

Waving that off, he said "I didn't want you to be mad at me anymore so I came over to ask you if you were with Malacca?"

"He's a fool," Bar said, as him and Twin continued to laugh.

"I ain't hollerin' at Malacca so do you," I tightly replied, wishing he would get the fuck on.

"How can you still be mad at me?" he innocently asked. "I told you."

Cutting him off, mainly because now definitely wasn't the time for this, I said " I'm not mad at you. I got you back. I took 'Lani from you so I'm cool."

"Lani?" he asked, a confused look on his face. "Lil' shorty I was diggin' right before I came home?"

"Yeah," I replied, a smirk now on my face. 'Lani compared to Trish was like a six compared to a dime. 'Lani was like that. I mean like that, and as soon as I found out that was his bun-buns I not only smashed her, I took her right when he was coming home so that when he made it to the halfway house I had my dick all of the way down her throat while he was trying to come over her house. I'd even went so far as to move in so he couldn't get released there on supervised release.

"Okay, well I guess that makes us even," he said, and then turned and looked at Bar. "What did he do to you for puttin' a baby up in her?"

"Oh shit!" Dog exclaimed, and everybody fell out laughing at the table. I mean, they were so loud that everybody in hearing distance was looking at us wondering what was going on.

"I'm with yah'll for the night," he said.

"Fuck no!" I tightly exclaimed, wanting this him as far away from me as possible. He was on some dumb-clown shit right now, and I hated being clowned.

CHAPTER 16

SASHA:

Dancing like that for a hour was tiring. There wasn't any moves or nothing, just hands waving in the air or holding on to whomever you were dancing with. It was fun and exhilarating, though I was glad, it was over. We would be dancing in twenty-minutes, and believe me a five-minute dance took a lot more energy than you might think. Especially when timing came into play. Finally making it back to VIP, me and Bree came through the velvet-rope to the sound of loud laughter, and we looked and saw that it was coming from Jet Life's table. By the time we made it to our table, which was right behind theirs, the laughter had died down, but whatever they had been laughing about still had Landra and Malacca smiling.

"Yah'll didn't dance?" I asked, seeing that neither one of them were sweating.

"Not in the middle of all of that," Malacca replied, face twisting up slightly as she shook her head.

"You know I don't dance," Landra replied, which was true. She never danced when we went out. She was the designated table holder and drink watcher.

"What were they laughing about?" I asked, nodding my head towards Jet Life's table.

"Come and find out," a voice I didn't recognize said from over there.

"Sure better be funny," I said, looking in the direction of the voice and seeing someone I didn't recognize, though he was cute to be honest with you. Especially with his little three-sixty waves.

"I'm definitely good at that," he said, as I walked over to their table. "Why don't yah'll come over here and sit with us."

"This ain't your table," Jet-Life said, mean muggin' him.

"I have my own table," I said smiling. "What's your name?"

"E-Neal," he replied, and added "don't mind him. He's been mad at me since I beat 'em up in the fourth-grade." Smiling, I looked at Jet-Life who was fighting to conceal the fact that he was staring daggers at him.

"You're a sack of shit," Jet-Life said, slightly shaking his head.

"I smell good though," E-Neal playfully retorted, and stood. "But since you won't bring your friends over here can I come over there with yah'll?"

"Depends on who you're coming to see," I replied.

Leaning forward, he said in my ear "Malacca. Make that happen for me."

"Drinks on you?" I whispered back because I didn't want Jet-Life to hear. I had absolutely no intentions of using the two-hundred dollars he gave me to buy drinks. A woman never bought her own drinks in a club full of men.

"Bottles," he replied.

"We'll be back," I said to everyone, and took E-Neal's hand and led him towards our table.

"Drop that 'em off and come on over here," Jet-Life said.

"I have to get ready to dance," I said.

"He's just jealous because I'm holding your hand," he said, and they laughed at their table.

"You's a fool," Herm stated.

"Malacca, do you know E-Neal?" I asked, as we came to my table.

"For too long," she replied, rolling her eyes.

"Damn, don't play me like that," E-Neal said as he released my hand and went over to stand beside her.

"Boy, you know I've got a man," Malacca said, which was part true and part not true. She had a man, but he wasn't much of a man so at times she didn't act like she had one at all. Especially when she was in Morgantown. But then everybody acted like they were single in Morgantown.

"A temporary problem," he said, and pulled a chair back and sat down beside of her. "Let me get yah'll something to drink. Let's get a couple of bottles over here."

"Don't be thinking you're getting any," Malacca stated, while rolling her eyes.

"You can't just give a me something that good once and not expect me to come back for more," he said, and all of our mouths hit the floor, and they busted out laughing at Jet-Life's table because he must have said it loud enough for them to hear.

"You are so wrong," Malacca tightly stated. "That was a long time ago."

"Ain't nothing long about three-years," he said, smiling.

"Boy, I've got a man and you can't stay out of prison so let's not even go there," she said, turning her nose up at him. Wow, I said to myself, she must actually like him.

"Don't worry about the little things pumpkin," he soothingly said, and patted her arm.

Shaking my head, I figured this just might be one of those nights that we talked about for quite some time to come.

CHAPTER 17

K-KUTTA:

After everything was set and ready, Diamond Cut had the girls sit over by her booth and me and Jet-Life go to our table off to the side. Because this was, Sasha's call-out Diamond had decided that they would go last. She had the other three-groups pick a number to decide the order, and the white-girl group, Next Up, was first, my girls were second, and the three-girl sorority group from West Virginia State were third. Sasha and her girl would be batting clean up.

"Here," Diamond Cut said, and handed me a microphone. "After each group performs I'll turn it on for the two of you to give your scores."

"Can we give our opinions?" Jet-Life asked.

Smiling, she said, "go ahead, but try to keep it brief."

Picture that, I said to myself and grinned as she headed back to the D.J, booth.

"You ever did one of these before?" Jet-Life asked.

"Not a dance-contest, but I be having to watch my dancers' routines, and work with them to rehearse for my shows," I replied.

"Your girls like that?"

"They're cool," I replied, which was true. I used them for shows that paid twenty-five hundred and less, which were most of the shows that I did unless I got a call-up from a major to mid-major artist doing a show somewhere around

West Virginia that needed me as part of their opening act. I may have been underground, but I averaged around four of those a year, which was cool. I'd even done some openings in Atlanta for my dude who I won't mention.

Turning off the low-playing music, Diamond Cut said, over the loudspeakers, "Bitches Night Out is proud to present The Call-Out. I know all of you have been eagerly awaiting the contest so I won't keep you waiting any longer. Our first act is a group known as Next Up. Let me present Melissa, Diane, Eva, and Katie."

As the four-girls came out to the dance-floor, I had to admit I was impressed with their outfits. I hadn't paid them much of any attention while Diamond Cut had everybody back by the booth getting everything situated, but their outfits said they just might be on point. Two of the four had on black halter-tops, white cargo-pants, black sneaks, with white bows in their black hair. The other two had on white halter-tops, black cargo-pants, white-sneakers, with black bows in their blond and red hair.

Coordination was the key, and maybe me and Jet-Life had misjudged this group by tossing them off to the side as a waste of some good time. They opened to Rihanna's "Talk That Talk," featuring Jay-Z, and their opening moves were coordinated as they did that little two-step dance in place. As Jay started rapping, they spun and faced us and the redhead stepped forward and started rapping Jay's lines while the three-girls behind her did a nice little routine.

225

And the little redhead chick had the facial features and the hand-gestures to go right along with it. She was doing it. They had their moves down pat, but they weren't dancers. Don't get me wrong they could dance for white-girls, but this wasn't a dance group. If I had to guess this was a girls-group. One I hadn't heard about before.

My guess was confirmed when, as soon as Jay's verse was done, Ke$ha's "Tik Tok" came on and they did the girly running slowly, with their heels kicking up high, as they switched positions and the blond was now in front and they faced the crowd. She did the KeSha performance, and their routine was distinctively white girl where before it had some black moves in it. I was liking how they switched it up. That was a bonus for them, which showed their range of dance moves. The only problem they had was one of the black-haired girls were like a half a second behind on her moves and that wasn't good.

They finished it up with Kevin Hart's "Baller Alert," featuring Migos, and T.I., and this time the two black-haired girls came to the front and performed like they were the Migos, finishing up when the Migo's initial verse was over. When they finished, the crowd loved it, and gave them a loud applause. Okay, most of the crowd was white, but don't take that like what they did wasn't like that, because it was.

"Okay, okay, okay," Diamond Cut said, calming the crowd down. "That was Next Up, and by the look of things we may be hearing from them sooner rather than later.

Now, let's see what the judges have to say about their performance. K-Kutta, what did you think?"

"I'm a be real with you," I said, and paused so I could lean forward and put my elbows on the table. "I thought yah'll was wasting our time until you jumped it off. The performance was cool, even though you're not a dance-group. Yah'll need to work on your timing a little bit more, but I'm a give yah'll a eight," I said, and handed the mic to Jet-Life.

Taking the microphone, he said "can yah'll sing?"

"Yes," the blond girl replied. "That's what we really do."

"Cool, cool," he stated, thinking what I was thinking as well. If they really could sing, something might actually come of this. "I'm a be real with you, the dancing was alright. It was more like a performance instead of a dance-contest. So what I'm a do is give you a eight with my dude because you did hold it down. I thought yah'll was going to flop to, but you surprised me."

"Sixteen it is for Next Up," Diamond Cut said, and the crowd started clapping. "Our next act's dancers who have appeared in a few videos, and done quite a few shows. Honey, Lucky, and Kamari."

CHAPTER 18

JET-LIFE:

Word, I wanted to give them like a six, but I rocked with the big homey and gave them an eight because it really wouldn't matter. They wasn't going to win anyway. If they could sing, they should have found a talent show to get involved in. This was dancing, and that shit they were doing wasn't even sexy on the real.

As they left the floor and went back towards the D.J. booth, I leaned over so I would be close to K-Kutta's ear and said, "I gave 'em an eight because of you. I was gone six they ass."

Laughing, he said "I figured that," and I leaned back over as his girls came the floor. I knew this was going to be way better than the last one so I leaned forward on the points of my elbows so I could focus.

As "I Got the Keys," by DJ Khalid, featuring Jay-Z & Future, came on I started bobbing my head. I fucks with Future. That's my dude so much, so that whatever he was on, I'm on. Shit, he was the reason I tried shrooms on the low. As "808 Mafia," sounded off they got to rocking. From the gate, you could tell they were way better than the white-girls. As one, their right arms went straight out and their left went to their hips as they crouched a bit. That's when their hips came to life and all of them started rotating their round mounds in a circular motion. One that was mesmerizing as hell. Especially since all of them had some super-fat asses.

Well, the white-girls was super-fat, but the other two were round and nice as hell. They were pushing them coochie-cutter shorts to the max.

I personally spent most of the performance watching Kamari's fine ass. She kept hitting me with the eye contact as she either bit her fingertip or bottom-lip. And every time she had that come and get it look on her face. A look that had me locked and loaded. And I mean locked and loaded. I was hard as hell watching her little sexy-ass put her thing down. All I could think about was what it would be like to tap that because she needed some Jet fuel in her Life.

When they were finally done, the crowd gave them their dues with loud applauds. Every dude on the front-row had that look on their faces. A look kind of like the one I had. The difference was that I wasn't hoping I was going to hit I was going to hit. The only question was when. I was after Sasha yah dig? Leaning back over until my mouth was next to K-Kutta's ear, I said "what's up with the red-bone?"

"She like that," he replied, letting me know that he had hit.

"Put me in the game."

"Consider it done," he replied. "She gone bring you your demonstration later."

"Thank you, thank you, thank you," Diamond Cut's said, as the crowd continued to applaud. "Calm down so we can see what the judges have to say about their performance."

"You wanna go first?" K-Kutta asked me, extending the mic to me.

Taking the mic, I said "Jet-Life up in this bitch!" and the crowd responded with a resounding "Jet-Life!" though most said it over and over a few times. They did love to pay tribute to yah boy because I was like that. "Alright, I'm a be real. That shit was like that. Yah'll did that," I said pointing to Kamari's fine ass. "I wanna give yah'll a nine, but that was better than a nine, but I've got to hold a ten back in case someone comes through with something better than that so what I'm a do is give yah'll a nine-in-a-half."

"That was smooth," Diamond Cut's said, as I passed the mic to K-Kutta.

Bringing the mic back to my lips really quick, I said "I ain't trying to have no tie. Somebody gone get this money and I'm a get back to partying. I ain't even smashed nothing yet," and K-Kutta fell out laughing as I extended him the mic.

"That you could've kept to yourself," Diamond Cut's good naturedly said, and quite a few people laughed.

Taking the mic, K-Kutta looked at me and said "you's a fool dog." Looking back at the girls, he said "I'm a tell you what. I ain't got no choice but to give yah'll a ten. That was smooth how all of that flowed together. Yah'll did that."

"Nineteen-point five," Diamond Cut's said, and the crowd applauded the score. I know quite a few of them were applauding my logic as well. Wasn't going to be no ties. When Sasha and Bre was done, this was over. It was time to party.

CHAPTER 19

K-KUTTA:

We're going to skip past the broads from State. They turned out to be what we thought the white-girls would be. A flop. I gave them a seven on the strength, but Jet-Life gave them a five and a tongue-lashing for wasting his time coming out here drunk and on some dumb shit.

When Diamond announced Sasha and Bre, they both brought their chairs out and sat them about fifteen-feet apart. Coming to the table, Sasha said "can I see your microphone?"

"Here you go," I replied, and handed it to her.

Turning it on, she tapped it a couple of times to make sure that it was on and then said, "for our performance tonight we're going to need two people."

"I'm game," a short, slim, brother said while stepping out of the front line and on to the dance-floor.

"Thank you," she sweetly stated, and then proceeded to kill his hopes. "But we already have them. Would Bar and Cutty come up here and have a seat please?" she said, and looked towards VIP.

"What the fuck did she pick them for?" Jet-Life asked in a voice just loud enough for me to hear. Like me, he was probably thinking that she was going to choose us.

"I don't even know who they are," I replied, which was true. At least it was until I finally saw them coming through

231

the crowd and on to the floor. I was introduced to them at his table earlier.

"Them," Jet-Life muttered.

"I don't know," I replied, wondering the same thing. Shit, if the chairs were any indication of what was to come they were about to get a nice little dance. I'd of definitely been game for that.

"I told you," Cutty said, pointing at Bar as they walked towards Sasha and Bre.

"Quit crying," Bar said, smiling.

"How can we help you beautiful?" Cutty asked Sasha.

"Have a seat and enjoy the show," she replied, and motioned towards the chair.

"You ain't gotta ask me twice," Bar said, as Bre extended her hand to him and he took it and followed her to the chair, the whole time looking at her butt. Taking Cutty to the chair Sasha let him get seated and then brought me the microphone back. Handing it to me, she said "enjoy the show," and winked.

"I'm there," I stated, taking the microphone from her.

"This shit better be right," Jet-Life said, and I knew him well enough to know that he wasn't feeling not being chosen to sit in that chair.

"Isn't it always?" she asked, and winked at him and turned and headed back to stand beside Cutty.

As they assumed their positions, Sasha on Cutty's left with her hand on his shoulder, and Bre on Bar's right with her hand on his shoulder, Diamond said "this is what we've all been waiting for. Ladies and Gentleman, I...AM...SASHA...FIERCE!"

As her words died down "Diva,"by Beyonce, came on and the show was on. And, for the first two-minutes, they gave the crowd exactly what they came for. They killed it. If there were three of them I would have sworn that Sasha was Beyonce she was so on point, and that's not taking anything away from Bre. For them to kill it she had to be on point as well, but Sasha was somewhere else with it. Her moves wasn't just crisp they were perfect. Like Bey dancing with her dancers. Bre was like the dancers and Sasha was Bey.

As "Diva" went to the second-chorus, it faded out and "Video Phone," by Beyonce, featuring Lady Gaga, came on. With Sasha and Bre about seven-feet from Bar and Cutty they both turned and faced them. Raising their right foot so it was on its tippy-toes, their left-hand went to their hips and they started snapping their fingers in unison with the song. That took some work to get that down just right, but anything less from them would have been uncivilized.

Backing up some as Bey came in they performed their routine for Beyonce's verse, killing it again. Even when they started dancing with each other, they were still in unison, though they were a bit freaky with it. The crowd loved it, and I was right along with them. And then, with Sasha's hands all over Bre's breasts, the music stopped and they froze in place right on cue.

I thought it was over until Nikki's voice came in on "Feeling Myself," by her featuring Beyonce. And then their heads snapped towards Bar and Cutty with that look that women gave us when they're hungry for what we've got. And that's when we all saw why they'd asked Bar and Cutty to come up on the stage. For the a minute and a half they took it all of the way to the strip-club and gave them lap-dances that we would all remember for quite some time afterwards. Literally.

CHAPTER 20

SASHA:

As the music finally ended, I finished on Cutty's lap with my arms wrapped around his neck. I knew way before the crowd went bananas that our performance was flawless. But the crowd going nuts was definitely an added bonus. Before I stood, I gave him a kiss on the cheek and then helped him stand, even though I know he would have much preferred to sit for a few more minutes. I had really worked him up. With my arm around his waist I guided him over to where Bre stood with her arm around Bar's waist, and we all bowed.

When we leaned, back up I gave him another kiss on the cheek, and then went to give Bre a hug. "We did it!" I hollered as we embraced.

"We killed it!" she happily stated, her arms tightly around my neck.

"Alright everybody," Diamond said, though we could barely hear her. It was just that loud in here. "Let's see what the judges have to say about that performance."

"Ten, ten, ten, ten, ten, ten," the chant went up until it became a roar. A roar that was music to my ears as it went on and on and on. It just seemed like they kept chanting it over and over for well over a minute. When I turned to look towards the D.J. booth, I saw K-Kutta and Jet-Life in the process of standing. They both raised their hands in the air and splayed their fingers wide, indicating a ten.

"It's official! The judges have both given them a ten!" Diamond said, and it got even louder as they drowned out the rest of what she was saying.

After about a minute Jet-Life started hollering over the microphone for everyone to quiet down as him and K-Kutta made their way up to where we stood. By the time they reached us the noise-level had went down some, even though it was still loud. You could now hear chants of "Jet-Life" in the crowd.

"Alight, this was real, but we've got to end this one the right way. First," he said, and paused to go in his pocket and take out a rubber-banded wad of money. "Three-stacks," he stated, and tossed me the money.

Catching it, you know I had the biggest smile on my face ever. I don't know if I'd ever had that much money in my hands, at one time that was mines. True, half of it was Bre's, but it sure felt like it was all mines at the time. "Thank you," I said, though I just mouthed it because it had gotten loud again.

"Thank you," Bre said as well.

Nodding his head to us, he said "you're welcome." Looking behind us to the dancers in the back, he said "aye, the rest of you all come up and do that bow thing for everybody so we can end this on the right note. This shit was real so let's end it how we carried it," he said, and motioned the other dancers who were still in the back to come up with us.

As they came up Bar and Cutty stepped over beside K-Kutta, who was off to the side of Jet-Life and shook hands with them. When the other girls came up we all linked arms around each other's waists and bowed to a round of thunderous applauds.

CHAPTER 21

JET-LIFE:

"It's time to get this party back crunk!" Diamond said, and everybody started cheering. "And there's no better way to do that than with a performance by none other than K-KUTTTTAAAAHHHHHHH!" she loudly stated, and I tossed him the mic and stepped off to the side with Bar and Cutty as his girls went to stand behind him. The rest of the girls, including Sasha and Bre, went to stand behind them so that there would be nobody between him and the crowd.

"H-Town stand up!" K-Kutta said, and tossed up his customary "H" that he made by raising his index and pinky-fingers, while lowering his ring and middle finger until they were straight and bringing his thumb up to meet them. "Charleston, are yah'll ready to get tuned up with me?" he asked, and the beat to his song, "Tuned Up," came on as the people said they were.

"I, I got that drank in my cup, drank in my cup. I, I, I got dat drank in my cup, loud in my pocket. Lou-Lou. I got that drank in my cup, loud in my pocket... Ro-Ro-Rollin like a wheel, takin' off like a rocket. Ro-Ro-Rollin like a wheel, takin' off like a rocket," K-Kutta rapped.

And you know I had my hand in the air rapping right along with him. This was my shit, even though Kat Von D was my favorite song of his. But this was that club banger that fit in especially for this type of crowd. Because there had to be, a gang of people up in here *rollin' like a wheel.*

"I'm tuned up like ah rari, on green like... a safari. I should a been ah..ah.. Marley, stay chromed up li-like a Harley," K-Kutta went in, and the party was back up and jumping as he ripped the first-verse with his sick-ass flow. For the life of me, I couldn't understand why he never hit big the way he killed it.

As everyone started dancing you know I couldn't just sit there with Bar and Cutty and bob my head with my hands in the air. That just wasn't my style. Especially since right behind him, I was looking at a collection of bad hoes, all of which needed some Jet in their Life. Looking at Sasha I didn't even wait for her to make eye contact with me, I just took off and circle around the back of K-Kutta and his dancers. She was standing beside Bre and one of the broads from State and they were mainly two stepping.

When I circled around the dancers, the white-girls were the first ones I saw and I flashed them my customary-grin as I moved on down the line. When I looked back up Sasha was looking at me and I could tell by the look on her face that she knew I was coming for her. At least that's what I thought I was doing until she nudged Bre and nodded her head towards me and they looked back at me and smiled. The next thing I knew I stopped in front of Sasha, and Bre circled around me and we started getting it in. And then some more of the dancers came over and we were all getting it in. I think we even got in the way of K-Kutta's dancers because I looked up and thick-ass Lucky was on my right and I turned and gave her some Jet-Fuel to get her life right.

We rocked the whole song like that, and he did the extended version of it. When the song ended, we all reluctantly stopped. You know I looked at Diamond like she'd lost her mind for not keeping it going, but the big-homie had to say something after his performance.

"Good lookin' on the love," K-Kutta said, and raised his hands and formed the "H" again. "Now let's all get tuned up in this bitch. Diamond crank this bitch back up," he said, and she did exactly that. And no, sooner than the beat came in the party went from a dead standstill to crunked. I had a gang of hoes around me, a few of my niggas in the vicinity incase the haters wanted to hate, but all I had eyes for was Sasha. No matter who I danced with, she wasn't going anywhere. That was me for the night, tomorrow night, and as many nights afterwards as I could fit in. Shit, if her bedroom game was like that I might go ahead and get that divorce I'd been contemplating for a minute now.

CHAPTER 22

K-KUTTA:

As "Just For The Night," By Migos, featuring Chris Brown, came on the velvet ropes that had been holding the crowd back was disregarded as the party went from a standstill to full tilt just like that. And everybody on the front-row wanted to party with us, so the poles holding the ropes were pushed down and here they came.

Before I could even think to fall back to the D. J. booth, I was surrounded by a bunch of black shorties. Now I'm not really the dancing type. Me on the dance floor just wasn't happening. I'm a fat-boy who's pretty much never caught without an all-white hand-towel to keep the sweat off of my face when I'm in hot places. I say that so you can understand that when "I Am Your Leader," by Nicky, Cam, and Rosay, came on I was sweating like a stuck pig. But I had a fatty grinding on my boy, pussy on each hip, titties on each shoulder, and a bad bitch on my back so it was all good. I was getting it in with my two-step reppin' for the fat-boys.

When "679," by Fetty Wap, featuring the Remy Boyz, came on, I started looking for a way out. A five-minute performance, and ten-minutes of dancing had yah boy breathing super-heavy, yah dig? And no, I'm not that big, but I am that out of shape. But I was pressed in real tight, and all I could see was dancing everywhere, which wasn't far since the lights that had just shined down on this part of the dance-floor were now off. I even tried turning in hopes of seeing a way back to Diamond's booth, but wasn't nothing happening.

Twenty-minutes later, "*Jumpman*," by Drake & Future, came on and I stopped dancing. Grabbing the girl in front of me, I told her that I needed to get back to V.I.P. I was cool with dancing at that point, though everybody else kept right on getting it in. I had to say it two more times before she finally caught on to what I was saying, but when she did, she took my hand and led the way, after motioning for everybody to follow.

It took like another ten-minutes to finally get there, and when we did, I needed a sit down. I had enough strength to drop them off at a table near where we were all sitting, order them drinks and me another bottle, and then head over to where E-Neal was sitting with Malacca because all of my peoples was gone, and how could you blame them? If you liked to dance this was the party of all parties, and that was still me the dent even though they played a pop song after every two or three hip-hop songs.

"Gad damn big homey," E-Neal said, looking up at me as I plopped in a chair a few seats down from him. "You look like I might need to bring you back."

Smiling, I said "let me go," and we all laughed.

"You looked good," Malacca said, and added "though you look like you're about to die now. Would you like some water?" she asked, while reaching for a water bottle.

"They tried to kill me," I replied, while nodding my head.

"Who, them?" E-Neal asked, and looked over to the shorties I had with me, while taking the water bottle from Malacca.

"Yeah," I replied, and dabbed at my face with the hand-towel. "They trapped me out there and I couldn't go nowhere."

Laughing, E-Neal said "shit big homey, you had four of 'em on you. That's a hell of a way to go," he added, smiling.

"Nasty ass," Malacca stated, while rolling her eyes. Taking the bottle from him, I uncapped it and took a long hit. I needed that. "Thanks," I said to Malacca.

"You're welcome, "she stated.

"Why aren't you out on the floor?" I said to E-Neal.

"Because she's too fine to dance," he replied, and blew her a kiss.

"You are so full of shit," she stated, though she was smiling.

"You're going to get me kicked out of the house for this one," we all heard, and looked up and saw Bar and Cutty coming down the aisle. "Did you see all of them people who were recording that shit on their phones?"

"Shit, all you had to do was get up," Bar replied.

"Get up?" Cutty asked, and stopped to put his hands on his hips and look at Bar like he had lost his mind, as Bar sat down.

"What's up," Bar said, as he sat.

"How are you going to say some stupid shit like that?" Cutty asked, and slowly shook his head. "That shit just sounded dumb as hell."

"Yeah, big homey, that did sound dumb as hell," E-Neal said.

"Why don't you mind your business?" Malacca asked, and then reached out and smacked him in the back of the head.

"Yeah, I'm with her on that one," Bar said, smiling like the rest of us as Cutty sat down beside of him. "What else did you want me to say?" he asked Cutty.

"That you're wrong as shit," Cutty replied, and then looked to me and said "I like that song big homey," How do I get that?"

"ITunes," I replied. "Or you can go to my page and get the link," I added, and gave him my real name so he could find me on Facebook, as well as my twitter link and instagram information.

"I'm on it," he stated.

"Here's your bottle sir," the waitress said, and sat a bottle down beside of me that was in a bucket of ice.

"Good lookin'," I stated. "We owe anything?"

"No, management said your drinks are on the house," she replied.

"Cool," I stated, and then took fifty-dollars out of my pocket and handed it to her. "Keep their drinks coming," I said, and nodded to the other table.

"I will," she said, as she took the money. "Anything else?" she asked.

"Bring us some more bottles of water," Malacca replied.

"Will do," she said, and left.

CHAPTER 23

JET-LIFE:

Making my way down the hall with this bad red-bone in tow whose name I couldn't remember, but for convenience sake let's call her Molly because that was the main reason she was coming along. That molly had my shit hard as a rock and I needed some relief before I busted on myself.

Coming to the bathroom-doors, I saw that quite a few people were hanging out talking. That usually meant that the bathrooms were packed inside, or everyone hanging around were tired as hell and needed a break. But fuck it, if it was packed, I knew how to make room. Especially since, I was going up in the girls bathroom to handle my business. I'd buy all of them drinks to get them up out of my way. I'm Jet-Life.

"Where are you taking me," she tittered, as she trooped right along behind me.

"In here," I replied, and headed towards the door to the females' bathroom, as people watched me pass. I know quite a few of them had to be wondering why I was going up in the girl's bathroom.

You can't go in there silly," she stated, and when I looked over my shoulder to give her that look that said I could go pretty much, where I wanted too, she was smiling so I took it that she was playing and not questioning my gangster.

"What are you doing?" some broad I didn't know asked, as I came abreast of the door that was just being opened by someone on the inside.

"Fuckin," I replied, and went in the opened door as the woman who had just opened it looked at me in startled-amazement. I don't think she'd ever seen a man blow up in the girls bathroom before. Well, if she stuck around long enough she'd see something else she hadn't seen before. Well, at least hear it. That was unless she opened the door to the stall. Then she could see whatever she wanted to. Fuck it, she could be next.

"Hey everybody," Molly said from behind me, and she actually had the nerves to wave at everyone who looked up at us in shock.

"Let me get one of these stalls," I said, and started walking past the row of stalls looking at the bottom of the door to see if I could see some feet at the bottom.

"Why?" a broad asked, and I followed the voice to a big titty brunette who was kind of cute.

"Stick around and find out," I replied, and went back to looking under stalls.

"She's nasty," someone muttered as I found an empty stall.

"Nah, I'm nasty," I said, and pushed open the door as I heard someone else say "that's Jet-Life."

"I'm nasty too," Molly stated.

Stepping off to the side, I let go of her hand and put my arm around her waist to guide her into the stall. and followed in behind her and pulled the door shut behind me and locked it.

"I'm nasty too," Molly again said, and started to turn around, but I stopped her.

See, I believed her. She was wearing one of those loose-fitting skirts that came down to right above her knees with no panties on. I knew this because, while we were dancing, she took my hands from her waist and put them under her skirt. When I felt the bare-cheeks, you know I had to make sure she didn't have a g-string on so I felt her pussy. As soon as I saw how wet she was it was on. I was looking for something to compliment this molly running through my system, and Molly was the perfect compliment.

"Put them hands on the back of the shitter and let me see how nasty you are," I said, and grabbed a handful of cheeks through the skirt. And in case you're wondering she wasn't holding like that back there, and I apologize for killing that image. She had some nice hips on her though, but the cheeks wasn't fat at all.

"What do you mean, like this?" she asked, and bent over and put her hands on the back of the toilet, while spreading her legs just a bit more.

"Yeah, just like that," I replied, and moved the fabric out of the way and got my first look at her bare-ass, which was a little bit lighter than she was. "Pussy any good?" I asked.

"I cannot believe he just asked her that!" some female out there loudly said. "Eww, I'm leaving."

"I can't believe you're ear-hustling, but here let me give you something to listen to," I said, as I reached in my back pocket and took out a rubber. "Watch how I work," I stated.

CHAPTER 24

K-KUTTA:

It took about three-shots of Cîroc, laced with molly, as well as some molly in my water bottle for me to get back right. But I was now back right and ready for some action. Nah, not no dance-floor action. That was a no go right there playah. I was ready to get my mack on, and I had four-shorty's waiting on me to holler at them.

"I'm a get up in a minute," I said, and pushed my chair back so I could stand.

"Where you headed, over there?" Bar asked, and let his eyes drift in the direction of the four-broads.

"Yeah," I replied.

"They all you or you need a cut partner?" he asked.

"Shit, I'm a snatch one of 'em and dip off to the side. The rest is on you," I replied.

"I am not going with you," Cutty said to Bar.

"Two's company, three's a crowd," E-Neal said, which made me laugh as I stood.

"You can stay with us if you want too," Malacca said to Cutty.

"He just likes to complain," Bar said to her. "He knows he's coming. He just wants to blame me when he gets caught."

"That's cause you're always the reason I get caught," Cutty said, and pushed his chair back as Bar did. "You're like the devil. You lead me into temptation."

"Good pussy'll do that," E-Neal stated.

Smacking him in the back of the head for like the tenth time, Malacca said "that's why you're not getting any. You can't keep your mouth shut."

"Don't bet on it," E-Neal said, and pushed his chair back. "Well, that is when I need to anyway," he added, and she rolled her eyes.

"Where do you think, you're going?" she asked, as I picked up my bottle and glass of orange juice.

"Shit, it's four of them and four of us," E-Neal replied.

"I bet you you're not leaving me here by myself," Malacca said, her eyes wide as saucers. Yeah, yah boy was trippin.

Wasn't no way he was supposed to be leaving nothing as fine as her by herself. Shit, if he went over to holler with us I was hitting her up on the low I already knew she was on my Facebook demonstration because I checked on the low when we were all at the table together. And since she had her phone with her, and it was more than likely linked to her page like mines was, I knew just how to get at her.

"You keep killin' me. What I'm a stay for?" he asked, and stood.

"I'm a leave yah'll to this one. I'm out," I said, not wanting to stick around for this conversation.

"Boy if you don't sit down," she replied.

"Well, since you asked," he replied, smiling as he sat.

"You did all of that for that?" Bar asked, and shook his head as I headed off.

"Play playboy," Cutty said.

"Mack your way and let me mack mines," E-Neal replied, and put his arm around Malacca's shoulder.

Going over to the girls table, I looked at the shorty that had led me through the crowd and crooked my finger for her to come with me. She wasn't the best looking of the three, but she was cute. And she'd done a lot of dirty dancing with me while we danced so I knew she was game.

"You're just going to talk to her?" one of them asked, her glass raised up just high enough to hide her lips, but not far enough to hide the dark-intent in her eyes. Intent that said she looked like she had go all up in her. And she looked a little better than the one I had just told to come here.

As the one I had crooked my finger at stood, I said, "let me holler at your friend real quick and then I'm a holla at you aight?"

"Alright," she replied, and reluctantly sat back down.

Looking back at her, I said "come on. Let me see what you're talking about," and you know she got up. "Yah'll hold my dudes down for me while I holler at your girl."

"Come on," she said, and put her arm around my waist and we were off to the table we had all of way in the cut. One that was dark and had seats that let us sit with our backs to everybody.

Pulling a chair out for her, I let her sit down and then I sat beside of her. I would've let her sit on my lap, but I wasn't trynah to take her to the room later. I was trying to bust her down in here so she needed to be sitting right beside of me so that she could lean over and work her magic.

"What's up, you trying to rock with yah boy?" I asked, and extended the bottle to her.

"I'm still sipping on this," she replied, and raised her cup.

"What's your name?"

"Ti' Amber," she replied, and added "I was wondering when you were going to ask."

"Shit, we just started talkin," I said, grinning.

"Hmmm, hm," she said as she raised the cup and slowly wrapped her lips around the straw and pulled on it. The whole time staring into my eyes all sexy-like.

"Damn, it's like that?" I asked, after she let the straw go.

"Like what?" she asked with a knowing grin.

Deciding not to reply to that dumb-ass question, mainly because I didn't play coy or any of that dumb-shit with groupies, I took a drink of my orange-juice. Setting the cup back down I took her hand and put it in my lap. "Does that feel like I'm trynah to play games with your cute ass?" I asked, as I used my hand to wrap both of ours around my semi-hard joint.

"So, am I going back to your room with you?" she asked, and started massaging it herself.

"Shit, I was trynah get some of what that straw was getting' now, yah dig?" I replied.

"Not out here like this," she replied, while slightly shaking her head. "But if you'll wait until later I can probably talk Daniel into coming with us," she said, and that got my attention.

"Which one is she?" I asked.

"The one you were going to talk to first," she replied.

"Cool," I replied, game for that. "I'll tell you what. Since we're going to take the party back to the room see if the rest of your girls wanna come. We can crank it right back up there."

"Alright," she replied, her hand still in my lap massaging me.

CHAPTER 25

SASHA:

We didn't get back to V.I.P until close to a quarter till three, and when we did, we were exhausted from dancing so much. Coming through the ropes, we left a lot of men on the other side of the ropes that wanted to come with us. Well, for that matter we left some women too.

Plopping down in a chair, Bre said "I am so tired."

"Here," H said, and picked up a bottle of water and handed it to her.

"She's not the only one thirsty," I said to Jet-Life, who was finishing the last of his chicken-wings.

Wiping his hands off, he grabbed his bottle of Ace of Spades and said "here," handing it to Lil' Lush to hand to me. "Fuck that water. This gone get you where you need to be."

"Give me some to," Bre said. "We haven't drank anything all night."

"Word?" Jet-Life asked, as Bre leaned forward to get two plastic cups from the stack in the middle of the table.

"They never drink before they dance," Landra replied, as Lil' Lush set the bottle in front of me.

"Should've told them hoes from State that," Jet-Life said, and added "they were gone."

"That shit was funny as hell," Lil Lush said.

"Yah'll hungry?" Jet-Life asked.

"Starving," Bre replied, and I had to admit I was looking at his chicken-bones wishing that he had a few more left. "Where's Malacca?"

"Using the bathroom," H replied, with a grin.

"And let me guess, E-Neal's with her?" I jokingly asked.

"You know it," H replied.

"Yah'll wanna eat here or when we leave?" Jet-Life asked.

"Where are we going after this?" Bre asked.

"IHOP, Hardee's, or do you feel like cooking?" Jet-Life replied.

"IHOP," I replied, mainly because I wasn't ready for the night to end. Nor was I ready to be cooped up in a house cooking. I was tired, but still wound up. "When are we leaving?"

"As soon as Mallaca comes back we can ride," he replied, and pushed his chair back. "Let me shoot over here and holler at Kut before we ride."

"Why is Bar and Cutty over there with them?" Bre asked, and I followed her gaze and saw them sitting at a table with three girls, two of which I knew. Both skanks.

"Trickin'," Jet-Life replied.

"That's exactly what they are," I said, and rolled my eyes.

"I'm coming," Bre said, and pushed her chair back and stood. And even I had to look at her wondering what was she on.

CHAPTER 26

Jet-Life:

With the party mostly over, we trooped into the front-part of the club at a little after three, where there was still a nice crowd. For whatever reason Bre was walking arm in arm with Cutty. I couldn't understand why, but I could care less. I had Sasha by my side so it was all good. And all of my niggas had something nice either with them, or waiting on them to swoop through and pick-up so if she wanted to bless that old nigga with some that was her business.

One thing for certain though her fine ass wasn't going to go home alone if I had anything to say about it. Her and Sasha in a three-some was definitely a thought I had entertained. Coming out front, I shook hands with the owner and he had a couple of words with Sasha and K-Kutta before we started down the sidewalk. K-Kutta and his people were going to the telly to keep the party going.

I knew what type of party that would turn out to be, and I was cool on that. They were about to have a freak-off and I didn't think Sasha or her girl would go for something like that so there was no in use us tagging along. They had like twenty or thirty hoes in tow so they should be good. Kamari kept giving me the eye, but I was cool. K-Kuttta had given me her number and said that she was game, but Sasha was on deck so that was something for tomorrow or the next day.

As we made our way down the sidewalk, we all heard someone holler, "Sasha Jones where the hell do you think you're going?" and most of us stopped. I stopped because he said "Sasha." When I looked in the direction of the voice I saw Lil' Bernie coming from the other side of the street and groaned. What the fuck did this wild ass want, I said to myself.

"Lil' Bernie you need to go on about your business," Sasha said, and I looked to see who was with him in case it was a problem. And he had two wild-childs with him. His cousin Lil' Markie, and Duval.

"Lil' Berne, chill," Lil' Lush said.

"Famo, I got this," Lil' Bernie said to Lil' Lush. "Bring yo ass here," he said to Sasha.

Man, fuck, I said to myself. There was no way in the hell I was letting him take my pussy like that, even though I wasn't strapped. Shit just wasn't going down like that. "My dude, she's with me," I said.

"So?" he asked, which was something along the lines of what I'd expected. We didn't mess with each other at all, even though we were both from the East. He was wild and messy, and I was cool on that. I'd learned after my first fed-bid that you couldn't get to the money being wild so I avoided dudes like I did broads who were rumored to mess with niggas that had that package.

CHAPTER 27

SASHA:

I couldn't believe Lil' Bernie was acting like this. Way back during the Christmas break, and last summer we had been an item, but we both knew there was nothing permanent so I couldn't understand why he was acting like this.

"So, she's with me," Jet-Life replied.

"For real?" Lil' Bernie asked, though it was pretty much a derisive snear.

"Have you lost your mind?" I asked Lil' Bernie, and I took a step off of the sidewalk and on to the street. My purpose of that was to put myself between him and Jet-Life because I could see Jet-Life's face tightening up after what Lil' Bernie had just said.

"Fall back," Lil' Bernie said to me, and then looked back to Jet-Life.

"No, you fall back," I said, and got all the way up in his face. "Who do you think you're playing with?" I asked, with crazy attitude now in my tone. "I am not your woman."

"How you gone fuck with him when you know I'm trynah holla?" he asked, now looking down at me.

"Excuse me?" I replied, though it was more like a statement than a question. Poking him in the chest, I said "the last time I checked you wasn't my man. Did I miss something?"

"You know what I mean," he replied, with just as much bravado. "When you're in Charleston you're mines," he stated, which was kind of the truth.

"Not anymore," I stated.

"Don't make me," he said, and stopped when I poked him in the chest.

Cutting him off, I said "I wasn't going home with him anyway. I'm going home with Bre. Those yesterdays are over. Men like you are why I mess with women. You think you can have your cake and eat it too."

"Go 'head with that dumb ass shit," he said, clearly not believing me. Either he had never known that I was bi-sexual or he wasn't trying to hear it. "You know what time it is. You're mines," he said, waving off what I had just said.

"You must not know who I am, so let me give you a wake-up call," I said, as I took a step back. "I... Am... Sasha... Fierce. And I belong to no man. But you all belong to me," I said, and looked from him to Jet-Life, and then back to him.

"That's a bad bitch there," Cutty said while nodding his head

"Amen to that," E-Neal stated.

"Preach," Lil' Lush said.

Turning from him, I walked pass Jet-Life and extended my hand to Bre, who had her arm linked in Cutty's. "Ready baby?" I asked.

"Let's go home momma," she replied, and took her arm from Cutty's and took my hand.

"Ladies, let's go," I said, and Landra and Malacca stepped out into the street with me and we all walked off with everyone watching. And I do mean everyone because the commotion had drawn everybody's attention.

CHAPTER 28

JET-LIFE:

Kiss my muthafuckin ass! I said to myself, as they all walked down the street and me and Lil' Bernie stood there stuck on stupid. And guess who was the first one to say something? Yep, E-Neal. He always had something to say.

"Noooooo," E-Neal said, and I didn't have to turn and see why he had just said that. "She was going to the 'telly with me," he stated, hands now on his head as he watched Malacca walking away.

"That was some cold-shit there," H said, and I was glad that JRoot wasn't there to see it. He would've clowned the shit out of me.

"Man, where they do that at?" K-Kutta asked, and him and his whole crew busted out laughing. Their laughter was so loud that you could hear it all up and down the street. Well, since there wasn't much of any talking going on that was easy to understand. Everyone had been ear hustling our situation anyway.

"Lil' Bernie, you just fucked up the pussy," E-Neal said, and I wanted to second that, though that wasn't all I wanted to do. I wanted to punch him in his mouth.

"Fuck that bitch," Lil' Bernie said, like me glaring daggers at her retreating back while silently praying that she would turn around and come back. That pussy had to be good to have him out here trippin like this.

"Fuck her, you just fucked up all of our pussy. Ain't that right Cutty?" E-Neal said.

"I was going home anyway," Cutty replied, and Bar busted out laughing.

"You ain't foolin' nobody with that," Bar said, still laughing. "She had you Bra. She had you."

"She did, I ain't even gone lie," Cutty replied, a longing look now on his face.

"Fuck," I stated, and turned to look at Lil' Bernie. "Is the pussy that good?" I asked.

"Fuck you," he replied, and started to turn and walk away, but I wasn't letting him get away that easy.

"Fuck me? You's muthfuckin' hater, " I said.

"Hater?" he asked, turning and looking at me like I was tripping. "What the fuck I got to hate on your soft-ass for?"

"Because you're not about this life," I replied, and at the top of my lungs I hollered, "JET-LIFE UP IN THIS BITCH!" And I shouldn't have to tell you what happened, but for those of you who still don't get the picture, the chant was taken up. Yeah, the "Jet-Life" chant.

CHAPTER 29

K-KUTTA:

As we laughed, I couldn't help shaking my head. She'd just stunted on them hard as hell. As I looked from Sasha, it was as if my eyes were drawn to Malacca. She was rolling too, which meant that E-Neal was out of the game. Time for a substitute, I said to myself. Heading back to the car, no, sooner than I shut the passenger door I went on my Facebook page and shot down to her name. Going to inbox, I sent her a message that said, "what it do?"

"With what?" was her reply.

"With you," I hit right back. It was around three-thirty and the time for playing had long-since passed so I couldn't understand why she was playing. Like she didn't know, why I was hitting her up this late for?

"What do you want to be up with me?" she hit right back.

"Have them drop you off at the Marriot," I shot back.

"I thought you had a girl or three with you?"

"You used the right word. Had. They were there because 'ole boy was all up in your ear, but now that's over put me in the game coach," was my next hit.

"And what would you do if you were in the game?"

Smiling, I hit back "I don't have to be at the shoot until around one so we have plenty of time for me to show you. Especially since I'm not tired."

"That wasn't an answer to my question."

"Does the pussy taste good?"

"As if you needed to ask," she replied, and added a sad emoji to go along with it.

"What about the ass?"

"Hmm."

"We gone need to shower and get all of that right cause I'm a worship you like the goddess you are."

"Don't have me standing out there waiting on you," she hit back, and this time the emoji was that of a cheerleader cheering.

"Hell yeah!" I exclaimed, when I saw her text. Hitting her back, I said "I'm a be there in five."

"What's up big homey?" Tip asked, as he wheeled us out of the parking spot.

"Just bagged something exclusive for the night," I replied.

"Excuse me?" Ti' Amber asked from the back seat with plenty of attitude in her voice.

"Aye, check this out," I said, and paused to turn in my seat. "I'm a have to take a rain-check on tonight."

"I bet you you're not about to play me out like that," she said, now pissed.

"I can't believe he just said that," Daniel said, sitting beside her. "How is he going to have us come with him and then tell us he's going to take a rain-check?" she asked, and added "like we're some type of hoe's or something."

"You are," I said, keeping it real with them, "but it's all good. I'm a get at ya'll tomorrow."

"I am not a hoe," Daniel said.

"Cool, cool," I stated, not wanting to keep going back and forth. "Yah'll can still come to the room and hang out though. It's still going to be crunked so chill and get your issue."

"I didn't come to hang out," Ti'Amber said. "I came to be with you. I cannot believe you're playing me like this."

"It happens," I said, and shrugged a shoulder. "The life and times of being K-Kutta. I mean, I am a star you know?" I asked, and turned back around and saw that Tip was fighting not to bust out laughing. Oh well, I said to myself, as I started envisioning what I was going to do to Malacca when I got her in the elevator. That pussy had to be fire the way she carried it. Hell, the way E-Neal was acting it had to be like that.

Merry Me

Marry Me

CHAPTER 1

As "*Top Off*," by DJ Khalid, Jay-Z, Future, and Beyonce', blasted through the sound-system of T-Wayne's, the new "it" upscale hip-hop two-story night-club in downtown Charleston, West Virginia, Shizza stood with a bottle of Ace of Spades in hand, riding the beat. At five-foot eight-inches tall, dark-skinned, and all of the way paid, he stood behind the second-floor railing of V.I.P. with the bottle raised in the air doing his little two-step as he envisioned himself in a Maybach with the roof chopped off.

Having consumed half of the bottle, which he'd put a quarter-ounce of Molly in when he brought it, he was good and wasted. So wasted that he wasn't even in the club right then. He was in Miami riding down the strip in a brand new Maybach that he had the top chopped off of.

"Look," Big Perm hollered, nudging Shizza and pointing to a group of young ladies standing at the first-floor bar.

Coming out of his zone, Shizza said "what's up bra," while lowering his arms and looking at him.

"Look at Tieka," Big Perm replied, still pointing.

Following his out-stretched finger, Shizza saw Tieka standing at the bar with her girls facing him looking out over the packed-crowd, and moisture flooded his mouth. Though she was a young-broad, she was a bad one. At five-ten she was all legs, though her athletic figure fit her just fine. Maybe because she was honey-brown, just how he liked them, and bad as hell. Like model beautiful.

"Damn bra," Shizza stated ,and looked over her form-fitting white dress that hugged every curve just right. He'd been trying to cut into her since he came home two-years ago, but nothing had ever come of it. He was at least ten-years older than her, which cramped his style somewhat. Though the only thing old he liked was his bourbon, she must not have been into older men because every time he sent someone at her to see what was up with him hitting her up she always shot him down. "I gotta get that," he said.

"Bettah not let Angel catch you up in her face," Big Perm jokingly stated, now smiling.

"Cut it out," Shizza stated, though he looked from Tieka to the crowd to see if he could spot his girl Angel.

The last thing he wanted was a scene, and she had no problems causing one if she thought that he was trying to play her. He knew that she was somewhere down in the crowd with her girls, all of which were from the West, because she hated being in V.I.P. But then again she wasn't above spying on him so he was now looking over the crowd to see where she was at.

"We goin' down?" Big Perm asked, wanting to be down in the midst of the party instead of up here in V.I.P.

"Bra, you know if I go down there they gone be all on me," Shizza replied. "You trynah have me up in here beefin all night?"

"Man, I'm 'bout to catch up wit' Big Paul and Tac. It's way too many hoes down there for this," Big Perm replied, and added "ole tender dick ass nigga."

"Fat-ass nigga, you don't even get no pussy," Shizza jokingly stated, and raised the bottle to take a healthy pull from it.

"Nigga," Big Perm said, while reaching in his pocket to take out his trick-knot. "As long as I keep a trick-knot big enough to choke a horse out I'm a fuck when, where, and how I wanna."

Wincing from the bite of the liquor, Shizza took a deep breath and then said "ole trick ass nigga."

"I'm rich," Big Perm gloatingly stated, while peeling a hundred and fifty-dollars in ones, fives, and tens, from the stack and tossing it out over the rail. "I'm a make it rain up in this bitch," he stated.

Laughing, Shizza watched the money fall for a few seconds before looking to where he'd last seen Tieka at. Seeing her still there, he saw one of her girls point to the money falling out over the crowd on the dance floor and saw her look up at them. Locking eyes with her, he grinned and raised the bottle in salute before taking a shot to the head.

CHAPTER 2

Coming down the steps to V.I.P., Shizza said "Don't get me in no trouble bra," as he stopped at the velvet-rope where he could see the full throng of people.

"You going out?" the bouncer asked, as he reached for the rope.

"Yeah," Shizza replied, biting back the witty retort that he wanted to say to the stupid ass question. Of course he was going out. What was the point in him standing there. "Bring yo big ass on," he said to Big Perm, who was following behind him, and stepped out on to the main floor where he saw a group of cuties standing there looking at him showing all of their teeth.

"Shizz," Big Perm said, stepping up beside him.

"Who are they?" Shizza asked, his smile lighting his face up as he wondered who these four beautiful women were. They couldn't be from Charleston because he knew most ever beautiful woman in the city.

"What do you mean who are they?" Angel loudly asked, as her five-foot, nine-inch, coke-bottle frame stepped around Big Perm's six-foot four-inch, three-hundred pound frame.

"Hey girl, where you been?" Shizza asked, his smile now even brighter if possible.

"What the hell do you mean 'where have I been?'" Angel asked with attitude, as she stepped in front of Shizza and poked him in the chest with her manicured finger. "You wasn't worried about where I was when you were trying to find out who your little jump-offs where."

"That's not what I said," Shizza replied, now looking at her like she'd lost her mind. Looking to Big Perm, he said "tell her that's not what I said," knowing that he would back him.

Cutting off what Big Perm was about to say, Angel said "I betchu if you lie for 'em I'm a smack the shit out of you," and pointed up at him to emphasize her point.

"Girl, cut it out," Shizza said, and pushed her hand out of Big Perms face. "It's a party girl," he said, and playfully grinded on her.

"Quit playing with me," Angel stated, and mushed him in the face to put some distance between them. "Don't be all up in my face and you wanted to know who the little hoes were that you were up there throwing money at."

"I told you that's not what I said," Shizza stated, now ready to go before she went from mad to pissed, and then to critical, which always resulted in a scene. "And that was big dummy lookin' for Jane to role with 'em for the night tossin money," he jokingly added, while nodding his head towards Big Perm.

"Lie for him," Angel threateningly stated, her finger still up in Big Perm's face.

Lightly swatting her hand out of his face, Big Perm said "I didn't hear what he said. You know the music was loud," before abruptly cutting off the rest of what he was saying.

"Lyin' muthafucka!" Angel yelled, smacking the shit out of him before either of them could stop her.

Because Angel was way shorter than Big Perm she had to step over in front of him, which gave Shizza all of the space he needed to effect his escape. "Jesus, take the wheel," he hollered, followed by the sound of a roaring engine as he sped off, getting little so that he could lose her in the crowd. He knew that Big Perm was a gentle giant so he wasn't too much worried about him wringing her neck. And as far as he was concerned Big Perm had brought it on himself by throwing that money out over the rail, which had brought her nosey-ass over to see what was going on.

Whirling around in time to see Shizza slide between two people and disappear, Angel started to go after him, but stopped. With having heels on she knew that there would be no catching him so she whirled back around and told Big Perm to take her upstairs. There, once she found him in the crowd, she'd be able to see what he was doing.

Dipping through the crowd while laughing, Shizza cut on to the dance floor because he knew that Angel wouldn't think that he was out there since he never danced. Not that he couldn't, he just didn't like to. Moving through the packed crowd on the dance floor while still slightly hunched over, he stopped to take a drink and paused with the bottle in mid-air as Patricia stepped in front of him with a sultry look on her face, just as "Street King's," by YFN Lucci, featuring Meek Mill, cut in and she started dancing.

Needing no further prompting, he pushed up on her fine red-bone thick to death ass. Word had it that she was now swinging both ways, and if it was true who her new boo was then he'd definitely be down with a creep with them. Who wouldn't want to mash-out with two bad ass dimes?

Dancing a couple of songs like that, Shizza took a step back to take a swig from the bottle, and then extended it to her. Taking it from him, as "Beef," by Tee Grizzy, featuring Meek Mill, came on, she turned and backed her butt up on him. Bouncing in tune with the up tempo beat, he was hard by the time she was putting the cap back on the bottle, which caused her to look at him over her shoulder with a raised eyebrow.

Busting out laughing, though keeping it firmly pressed to her backside, Shizza snaked an arm around her waist and plucked the bottle out of her hand with the other. "This my time," he said into her ear. "You been playin hard as fuck to get, now let me see what you workin with."

CHAPTER 3

"Where you been?" Taco asked Shizza, as he came over to the table where he sat with Big Paul and Big Perm.

"Trickin," Shizza replied, and flopped into the empty chair between Taco and Big Perm. Pointing at Big Perm, while looking at Taco, he said "bra, baby smacked the dog-shit out of that big dumb-ass nigga," and then busted out laughing.

"Who Angel?" Taco asked, grinning as Big Paul started laughing.

"Yeah," Shizza replied, smacking the table as he laughed harder.

Looking to Big Perm, Taco said "you didn't tell us that."

"Yo bra, that nigga had the dumbest look in the world on his face," Shizza stated, still laughing.

"How'd you know what I looked like?" Big Perm asked. "You took off and left," he sarcastically added.

"Shit, I gave Jesus the wheel and he sped me off," Shizza jokingly replied, and everybody fell out laughing.

"You're a fool," Big Paul stated, laughing along with everyone else at Shizza's crazy ass.

"I almost choked her out," Big Perm said.

"You a fool...," Taco said, and before he could say anything else, he saw Angel standing behind Shizza. "Bra, behind you," he stated, which caused everyone to look in that direction.

Whack! They all heard as Angel smacked the taste out of Shizza's mouth no sooner than his head was halfway around. Rolling with the smack, Shizza did the best thing he could under the circumstances and reached out and grabbed a handful of her dress and pulled her towards him even though his head was now turned back the other way. He knew enough to know that she was quick on the draw, and was probably drawing back to hit him again.

"Girl chill," he said, as he drew her to him and quickly pulled her on to his lap.

"Damn she smacked the shit out of you," Taco said, laughing.

"Yeah, see how that shit feels," Big Perm gloatingly stated, laughing and pointing at Shizza.

"I'm a fuck you up," Angel said, trying to get her arms free, but he kept holding her fast. "You all up in these bitches faces, playing me like I'm stupid."

"I wasn't in no bitches face," Shizza said. "Come on babe, chill. You drunk babe. Chill out," he added, while still fighting to keep her arms pinned to her side.

"I'm a chill after I fuck you up," she slurred out, still trying to get loose.

Knowing that the only way that he was going to calm her down was to kiss her, Shizza let one of her arms go and quickly grabbed her hair and molded his lips to hers, while she tried to hit him.

"Go ahead lover boy," Taco jokingly stated, laughing at their antics.

Taking a shot to the side of the head, Shizza wrestled her free arm down to her side, while deepening the kiss. He knew that no matter how mad she was at him, as long as he got her to kissing him she'd eventually calm down. As her arms stopped moving, her lips parted and he resisted the urge to stick his tongue in her mouth. He'd done that once before and she'd bit down on his tongue. That definitely wasn't something he wanted his partners to see. They would never let him live that down.

www.ingramcontent.com/pod-product-compliance
Lightning Source LLC
Chambersburg PA
CBHW022027240626
47154CB00007B/2297